Doing the right thing . . .

Summer kissed Austin softly. She tried not to think about the longing and sadness and regret churning inside her. She tried not to sob when one of Austin's tears dampened her own cheek.

She was being faithful to Seth. She was doing the right thing. She was being honorable and loyal and steadfast and true.

Sometimes doing the right thing hurt like hell.

"So long," Austin whispered as she pulled away.

She closed the door behind her so he wouldn't hear her cry.

Don't miss the other books in this
romantic series:

#1 June Dreams
#2 July's Promise
#3 August Magic
#4 Sand, Surf, and Secrets

Special edition Spring Break Reunion

Available from ARCHWAY Paperbacks

Summer

Rays, Romance, and Rivalry

Katherine Applegate

AN ARCHWAY PAPERBACK
Published by POCKET BOOKS

New York   London   Toronto   Sydney   Tokyo   Singapore

To Michael

AN ARCHWAY PAPERBACK *Original*

 An Archway Paperback published by
POCKET BOOKS, a division of Simon & Schuster Inc.
1230 Avenue of the Americas, New York, NY 10020

Produced by Daniel Weiss Associates, Inc., New York

Copyright © 1996 by Daniel Weiss Associates, Inc., and
Katherine Applegate

Cover art copyright © 1996 by Daniel Weiss Associates, Inc.

ISBN: 0-671-51039-8

First Archway Paperback printing July 1996

10 9 8 7 6 5 4 3 2 1

AN ARCHWAY PAPERBACK and colophon are
registered trademarks of Simon & Schuster Inc.

Printed in the U.S.A.

IL 7+

1

You Want Faithful?
Get Yourself a Dog.

I don't believe it. Summer wouldn't betray me this way."

Seth Warner cringed at the catch in his own voice. Was he at all convinced by what he was saying? Was she?

Diana turned away from his bedroom window. The pity in her eyes told him the answer.

"If she's hanging out with Austin," Seth persisted, "it's because they're friends."

"Maybe," Diana conceded gently. "But then why didn't she tell you about him?"

"Because . . . because she knew how upset I'd be. She didn't want me worrying when we were so far apart."

That made sense, he told himself. He was on

1

the West Coast. She was way out there in
Florida. Pacific, Atlantic. Disneyland, Disney
World. They were a bicoastal couple. This sort
of thing was bound to happen.

"Summer wouldn't do something like that.
She wouldn't."

She couldn't, he added silently. They were
engaged. That meant something. It meant
everything.

She just couldn't.

And yet not an hour before, when he'd tried
to call Summer in Florida, her roommate,
Marquez, had given him the answer he didn't
want to hear.

"Just tell me this," he'd practically begged
Marquez. "Is she with Austin?"

"Yeah, Seth," Marquez had answered. She'd
sounded far away and hazy. He'd wondered
whose side she was on—his or Austin's.

"Seth." Diana broke into his thoughts.
"Summer already did it once. Have you forgotten spring break?"

"But she told me about that. She's not the
kind of person who would keep a secret—"

"Not like you, you mean?"

The accusation stung. He still regretted last
New Year's. Not that Diana wasn't an incredibly
beautiful girl. Not that he wasn't still attracted

to her, even now, as she stood by the window gazing out at the darkening sky. But that had been just one time. It had been a mistake—a big, very regrettable one. Especially since Diana and Summer were not only roommates but cousins.

It was the kind of mistake that made the guys at work roll their eyes and shake their heads and say things like, "Man, whatever you do, don't ever let her find out, not if you want to live to see nineteen."

That kind of mistake. Major.

"You never exactly mentioned New Year's to Summer, did you?" Diana asked.

Seth closed his eyes and sighed deeply. "I know. I know. I'm a hypocrite."

"Well, then, so am I."

Diana went over to the bed and sat beside him. He could smell her perfume, exotic and spicy. A little mysterious, like her. Dark hair, dark gray eyes, an intense, almost scary kind of beauty. She was the kind of girl guys lusted after from afar but never had the nerve to approach. He still had a hard time believing that New Year's had ever happened.

She was so different from Summer. Summer, who always made him think of morning—light and hopeful and full of possibilities. Summer was sweet and genuinely good in a way Seth knew he could never quite be.

Diana touched his hand. "I don't regret what happened between us, Seth. Do you?"

Seth stared past her out the window. He didn't answer.

"She wouldn't do it," he said at last. "We're engaged, Diana. She's wearing my ring."

Diana took a long, slow breath. "I want you to know something, Seth. I didn't want to do this. I didn't want to come here and tell you these things. But in my heart I knew you deserved the truth. You deserve a whole lot better than this. A whole lot better."

She reached for her purse. Slowly she unzipped the little pouch.

When she took out the ring and held it in the air, all Seth could do was stare at it, mesmerized, as if she'd performed a fantastic, impossible magic trick.

It was Summer's ring, all right. The one he'd made payments on for months. The little rock had just about bankrupted him.

When he'd put it on Summer's finger that perfect night during the prom, he'd had to push the ring to get it past her knuckle. He'd been afraid, for one terrifying moment, that the ring was the wrong size. That his carefully orches-

4

trated evening was going to fall apart. Ejected from the game on a technicality.

But of course it had fit. He could still see, with perfect clarity, the look of astonishment in her blue eyes.

And now, through some amazing sleight of hand, there it was before him. Not on Summer's finger, where it belonged, but in Diana's hand.

"She hasn't worn it for a long time, Seth," Diana said. Her whisper was full of regret.

Slowly Seth began to put the pieces together. Diana had flown all the way across the country armed with pictures of Summer and Austin together. And with this ring, Summer's ring.

This wasn't magic. This was Diana at her calculating worst.He pulled his gaze from the ring to Diana.

"You certainly came prepared," Seth said angrily. "You brought everything but fingerprints, Diana. 'Gee whiz, Seth'"—he imitated her sultry, fake-innocent voice—"'didn't Summer mention Austin?' Why'd you even bother with the innocent act? Why not just trot out the evidence like the FBI?"

Diana looked away. She almost seemed hurt. Almost.

"I thought you liked innocent," she said. "It always worked for Summer."

Summer. Who had filled his dreams. Who had been his future.

Who was with Austin, he knew, that very moment. In Austin's arms. Kissing him, touching him . . .

Seth yanked the ring from Diana's grasp and threw it across the room. The satisfied smile on her face did not surprise him. In one swift move he pulled Diana down on top of him.

He could still hear the ring rolling slowly across the floor as they began to kiss.

2

Meanwhile, Back at the Ranch . . .

Summer could still hear the waves crashing slowly onto the sand as Austin bent down to kiss her.

It had been an hour since they'd left the beach and walked back to her front porch. An hour since she'd told him, finally and absolutely, that it was over between them.

His warm lips brushed hers. She backed away a step. "Austin—"

"It's my birthday, you realize," he said with just the hint of a smile.

"Under the circumstances, I don't think kissing would be a good idea."

"A harmless good-night kiss, nothing more." He ran a finger down her bare arm. The bright yellow porch light turned his dark eyes amber.

"I really don't think—"

"Okay, then." Austin hooked his thumbs into the pockets of his worn jeans. "I'm going to go for the last-ditch, cross-your-fingers, Hail Mary pass. The mark of a truly desperate man."

In spite of her resolve not to be further charmed by Austin, Summer laughed. "And that would be . . . ?"

"An appeal to your merciful nature—the pity kiss. It's the least you can do, Summer. You've just tried to end our relationship. On my birthday, no less."

"I haven't just *tried* to end it, Austin. I really have."

"I've heard that before, though, haven't I?"

"But I mean it this time." Summer crossed her arms over her chest. "I—" She paused when she heard footsteps approaching from the pool area in the backyard.

It was Blythe, a tall, stunningly pretty black girl who lived on the second floor of the building. Someone was with her, a girl Summer had never seen before. They were both wearing bathing suits, with damp towels wrapped around their waists.

"Hey, guys, how's it going?" Blythe started

up the steps, leaving wet footprints in her wake. "Hope we're interrupting something."

"You're not," Austin replied glumly. "Unfortunately for me."

"What a waste," said the second girl, eyeing Austin appreciatively.

"Down, girl, he's taken," Blythe warned. "Caroline Delany, this is Summer Smith and Austin Reed. Caroline's from Virginia. She and I used to be counselors at a summer camp there. I haven't seen her in ages."

"How long are you staying?" Summer asked, grateful for any reprieve from her conversation with Austin.

"Oh, a couple of weeks, a couple of months," Caroline replied. "As long as Blythe can stand me."

She had a sweet smile, Summer thought. With her short blond hair caught back with a little barrette and her slight build, she looked younger than the rest of them, almost vulnerable.

"I told Caroline if she gets on my nerves too totally, I'll force her to pick up my shifts at Jitters. That'll get rid of her," Blythe teased. "Hey, that reminds me. Marquez isn't working tonight, is she?"

"I'm pretty sure she has the night off," Summer said. "Why?"

"We asked her to join us down at the pool, but she said Diver was coming over. She seemed kind of down, so I went back to check on her about an hour ago. But when I knocked on your apartment door, no one answered. Guess she and Diver decided to go out."

"I thought Diver had to work late tonight," Summer said, frowning. "I hope Marquez is okay."

"She *has* seemed a little stressed out," Blythe said. "I mean, I hardly know the girl, but at work she's been either totally hyper or totally zoned, you know?"

"I know. I've been worried about her too. She's been on this major exercise binge. I swear I never see her eat anything anymore."

"Wish I had that problem." Caroline patted her rear. "But I never met a fry I didn't like."

The two girls headed inside. "There goes every man's fantasy woman," Austin said with a smirk. "Never met a guy she didn't like."

"*Fry,* you sleazebag. See how easy it will be to get over me? You're already scoping out the possibilities."

Austin's grin vanished. "Not likely, Summer. You're irreplaceable." He shook his head sadly. "You're making a terrible mistake, you know. How many guys are you going to find who'll say nauseatingly corny things like that? Out loud? In public? Even without being threatened with bodily injury if they don't?"

Summer took a deep breath. "This is the right thing for me, Austin. I feel good about this decision. I really do."

She wondered if she sounded convincing. She wondered if she herself was convinced.

The truth was, she didn't feel good about this decision at all.

The truth was, she wanted Austin. She loved Austin.

But she loved Seth too, and she owed him her loyalty in a way she didn't owe Austin. She'd made a vow to Seth. And if she hadn't honored it as well as she should have so far, well, maybe it wasn't too late to try.

Seth had loved her enough to place a ring on her finger. And if she'd accidentally lost the ring, well, maybe it wasn't too late to replace it.

With a remarkably similar one, she hoped.

"I'm not going to just walk away," Austin said. "I'm not going gently into that good night—" He groaned. "Damn. That's a bad sign. When I'm desperate, I start quoting poetry."

"At least it wasn't a dirty limerick."

Silence fell. Suddenly the air seemed suffocating, with its thick, sweet scent of jasmine and

11

heavy wetness. Night noises filled the emptiness—crickets and frogs thrumming, the ebb and flow of the nearby surf, the rustle of palm trees catching the occasional tendril of breeze.

Austin took her hands in his and held on too tightly. "Summer, look . . . I . . . what if I told you I need you right now?"

The lost, childlike sound of his words made her ache. His eyes shimmered with tears.

"Austin . . . don't."

"What I mean is—" Austin paused. "I can't lose you right now. I already feel like I'm losing everything."

His father. That's what he meant, Summer knew. Austin's dad had a hereditary illness called Huntington's disease. He was confined to a hospital bed, unable to communicate, slowly dying. Austin's brother had inherited the gene that caused the disease. Austin had recently been tested for it too. Fortunately, he'd been luckier than his brother.

"I will always be here for you, Austin," Summer whispered. "Anytime you need to talk—you know, about your dad or anything else—I'm here. It's not like we can't be friends."

"We *are* friends. Friends who happen to be in love with each other." Austin leaned against the porch rail. He stared past her into the velvety darkness.

He was so different from Seth, Summer thought. Intense, surprising, independent. Something about Austin told you he didn't give a damn what the world happened to be thinking about him. His looks just added to that impression: longish brown hair that refused to behave, a perpetual hint of beard, a couple of tiny silver hoops dangling from one earlobe, an ever-present and charming smirk.

And yet there was a wistfulness about Austin as well. Summer always had the feeling he'd lost something and was desperately trying to recapture it. What it was, she didn't know. He was still a mystery to her. An almost irresistible one.

Seth, on the other hand, was pretty much an open book. Steady, protective, reliable, completely faithful. He was the boy next door. She was the girl next door. And it seemed inevitable that someday they'd get married and have little kids next door of their own.

Austin squared his shoulders. He looked calmer, as if he'd come to some conclusion.

"Maybe this is a good thing." He said the words slowly, measuring each one. "I've often wondered if coming here to the Keys to be near you was a good idea. I talked myself into believing that if it was good for me, it would be good for you. . . ."

The cool, distant look in his eyes told Summer that he was already pulling away from her. Good, she told herself. That was what she wanted.

"But you deserve better than I can give you, Summer. I come with a lot of . . . well, limitations. I'm like one of those crappy plane tickets, full of restrictions, where you can only travel to certain places at certain times of the week . . . and for only so long."

"What limitations, Austin? I don't understand. What are you talking about?"

He shrugged. "Limitations. We'll let it go at that, all right?"

"You are not a crappy ticket," Summer said softly. "You are most definitely first-class round-trip to Paris."

"No. I'm more like one-way to Kalamazoo. On Greyhound. Sitting next to a guy who smells like bad cheese while he drools on your shoulder. But let's quit while we're ahead. This analogy is in danger of collapsing under its own weight. The point is, maybe this is all for the best." His tone was resigned and flat. He sounded deeply tired.

"Maybe Seth is the guy for you. I doubt it, but then, I'm biased."

For some reason Summer was reminded of the message Austin's brother had left on his machine earlier that evening.

"It gets easier after a while," he'd said, "really it does." He'd had the same resigned, weary sound that Austin had right at that moment.

She touched his arm. He gazed at her fingers on the taut muscle of his forearm and smiled a little. "So. One last pity pucker for the road?"

Summer kissed him softly. She tried not to think about the longing and sadness and regret churning inside her. She tried not to sob when one of Austin's tears dampened her own cheek.

She was being faithful to Seth. She was doing the right thing. She was being honorable and loyal and steadfast and true.

Sometimes doing the right thing hurt like hell.

"So long," Austin whispered as she pulled away.

She closed the door behind her so he wouldn't hear her cry.

3

Hard Questions, No Answers

Summer slowly climbed the three flights to the apartment she shared with Marquez and Diana.

It was a great place—a charming attic apartment in a Victorian house, complete with two porches, one overlooking the bustling main street, the other directly over a small pool in the backyard with the ocean a little ways beyond. The house was located right in the heart of Coconut Key, which boasted two great colleges and endless miles of pristine white beaches.

It was the perfect tropical paradise, except for one tiny problem: Austin. It was bad enough he'd moved to the Florida Keys to be close to Summer, but he even worked at a café on the bottom floor of her apartment building. How was she ever going to avoid seeing him?

It was way too easy to imagine the awkward encounters, especially when Seth came back from California. But it wasn't as though she could move. They'd just signed a lease for the summer. And Marquez and Diana loved the apartment.

It was impossibly complicated and impossibly sad. Summer sniffled as she fumbled for her key.

"Marquez?" Summer called as she unlocked the door. "It's me, and do I ever need a Chunky Monkey fix—"

No answer, but the lights and the stereo were on.

"Diver? Are you guys in the bedroom?"

Summer took another step. The apartment was eerily quiet. "Marquez?" she whispered.

The first thing she saw was the hand.

Marquez's hand, jutting out from behind the couch.

Summer gasped, and her heart shot into her throat. She ran to Marquez's side.

Blood trickled from a cut on Marquez's forehead. Her usually dark complexion was chalky. She was wearing her exercise sweats. A towel lay by her side.

Summer took her friend's hand. It was cool and limp.

Oh, God, please don't let her be . . .

Summer felt for a pulse.

Nothing.

She tried again, watching to see if Marquez was breathing.

Finally Summer found a pulse, saw a shallow breath.

The phone—where was Diana's cell phone? Their apartment phone hadn't been turned on yet. Frantically Summer dug under the couch cushions.

Damn it, where was the phone?

She sprinted to the hallway. "Blythe!" she screamed down the stairwell. "Call nine-one-one! Blythe!"

Blythe's door flew open. "What's wrong?" Blythe demanded. She was still in her bathing suit.

"It's Marquez! She's fainted! I think she was exercising. She must have passed out and hit her head. Call nine-one-one for me, right away!"

"It'll be okay," Blythe said calmly. "Go back to Marquez. I'll be right up as soon as I call."

Summer ran back down the hall to the apartment. She grabbed a blanket off the couch and gently covered her friend.

She looked so small. Tough, unstoppable,

crazy Marquez. Summer squeezed her limp hand. Marquez's arm was light, just a slender stick of bone. Summer hadn't realized how thin she'd gotten.

So thin, so quickly. Why hadn't she noticed? They'd all been so busy encouraging Marquez about her weight loss. Maybe they'd been too encouraging.

Blythe and Caroline appeared in the doorway. "They're on their way," Blythe reported. "I'll bet she just got light-headed working out, that's all."

"She'll be okay, Summer," Caroline said.

Summer brushed Marquez's thick hair away from her face. "I hope you're right," she whispered, but she wasn't nearly so certain.

Marquez? Can you hear me, hon?

She's been slipping in and out. Her BP's up. One-ten over sixty. Pulse is still a little thready.

Marquez? I'm Dr. Mary Lewis. Almost the same first name as you, although your friend tells me you don't use it. Open your eyes, Marquez. Do you know where you are?

Come on, Marquez. Stay with us here.

You hit your head, Marquez. You're in Fairview General, the hospital on Coconut Key. Sounds to me like you got a little carried away on the exercise bike and fell off and hit your head. Just took a couple of stitches. You won't even notice them. Marquez?

I haven't gotten anywhere with her, either. She hears okay, she just won't . . . Hey, you sure she fell off a bike?

That's what her roommate told the admitting nurse. Why do you ask?

Just something she said. The only thing, actually. Something about diving.

Hmm. I doubt it . . . I mean, her clothes were dry, her hair was dry.

Maybe I got it wrong.

Marquez? Listen, I need to ask you some questions so we can be sure we give you the right medications, okay? You need to help me out on this, Marquez.

Have you been taking anything? Drugs of any kind?

It's okay to tell us. We just want to help you, hon. And we can't help you unless you tell us the truth.

How about it? Cocaine, crack? Maybe some amphetamines? Speed?

Come on, Marquez. Work with us here. We're not the bad guys, okay?

We're getting nowhere. Where's that roommate of hers? Maybe I'll try her.

Waiting room, I think. Want me to get her?

I'll go talk to her. Give me a full blood workup, and let's keep Marquez here overnight for observation.

I'll be back later, Marquez. Maybe you'll feel like talking more then.

What's that? Did you say something, hon?

Something about diving again, I'm pretty sure.

Diving! Right. No diving for you anytime soon, kiddo. About the last thing in the world you need right now is more exercise.

4

Best Friends, Brothers, and Other Troubling Mysteries

*D*iver!"

Summer ran to meet her brother as he entered the waiting room. She hugged him, then pulled away, suddenly self-conscious.

"Marquez—"

"She's okay," Summer assured him. "I talked to the nurse a little while ago. They're going to keep her overnight, just to be on the safe side."

"Thank God. I was so scared." Diver sank into a yellow vinyl chair.

"The nurse said Marquez's doctor wants to talk to us, but then we can probably go see her."

Diver combed back his long sun-streaked hair. His dark blue eyes were clouded with worry. "I wish I could have gotten here sooner.

I must have broken twenty traffic laws on the way."

"My neighbor Blythe and a friend of hers drove me over. They're down in the cafeteria."

"Summer—" Diver hesitated. "Why does the doctor want to talk to us? Marquez just fainted, right? You're not keeping something from me, are you?"

"No, of course not. I don't know why she wants to talk to us." Summer sighed. "I've been kind of worried about Marquez lately. She's seemed so stressed out."

"Yeah. I've been worried too."

"But you know Marquez—you say one word to her and she bites your head off."

Diver leapt from his chair and began pacing the small room. "She's been exercising constantly, and she hardly ever eats. She never ate well. Marquez thinks a bag of Doritos and a Diet Pepsi is a well-balanced meal. But lately . . . I never see her eat anything."

He reached the end of the room for the second time and spun around. Summer almost smiled. She'd never actually seen someone pacing before. Her usually mellow brother looked like one of those anxious expectant fathers in a TV sitcom. Only there was nothing funny about this.

Diver took another turn. "Marquez means everything to me. If anything ever happened to her . . ." He glanced at Summer, then looked away.

Summer thought she saw guilt in his eyes. And why not? Why was it so easy for Diver to care about Marquez? Why, when it had been so hard for him to care about his parents—Summer's parents—and Summer herself?

A tall young African-American woman in a white coat, a stethoscope draped around her neck, strode into the waiting room.

"Summer Smith?" she asked.

Summer nodded. "I'm Summer. And this is my brother, Diver."

"Diver? Ah, so that explains it. Marquez was asking for you. I'm Dr. Lewis." She sat on the couch with a sigh. "Take a load off. I need to ask you a couple of questions."

"Marquez will be okay?" Diver asked.

"In the short term, yes." The doctor leaned forward, hands clasped on her knees. "Look, I won't beat around the bush. Does Marquez use anything?"

"Use?" Summer repeated.

"Drugs. Coke, maybe, or amphetamines? We're running her blood work right now, but she came in with the pulse rate of a hummingbird, and drug usage would fit with some of her other symptoms."

"Marquez would never use drugs," Summer said automatically.

Diver looked away.

The doctor pursed her lips. "Has she been exercising excessively lately, losing a lot of weight? Maybe bingeing and purging . . . you know, throwing up after meals?"

"She's been on a real exercise jag, yeah," Summer said. "And she's lost a lot of weight really fast. We've all told her a zillion times how great she looks—"

"I found some pills," Diver interrupted. His face was pale. "She told me they were just over-the-counter stuff, diet pills someone at work gave her. I made her throw them away. I figured . . . I thought she was okay."

"Well, she's not okay," Dr. Lewis said grimly. "Marquez could be on the road to a serious eating disorder. I'm going to give her the name of a support group that meets once a week here at the hospital. Your job is to encourage her to get some help, got it?"

Diver rubbed his eyes. "I told her how beautiful she was. I told her she didn't need to lose any more weight—"

"It's not about losing weight, Diver," the

doctor said gently. "For people with eating disorders, it's all about getting control over their lives. This is the only way they know to do it. Has Marquez been under a lot of stress lately?"

"Her family lost their house and business and moved to Texas. They were really close," Summer said. "And she didn't get into the college she wanted, and she caught her boyfriend in bed with another girl—"

The doctor cast a dark glance at Diver.

"No, not Diver," Summer added quickly. "Her *former* boyfriend. And she's been having money problems and working what seems like quadruple shifts."

"So the answer is a definite yes," the doctor said as she stood. "Look, it's important for her friends to be supportive, but in the end what Marquez really needs is professional help. Do what you can, okay?"

"We will," Summer promised.

"Can we see her?" Diver asked.

"Of course. Maybe she'll be a little more talkative with you than she was with us. They're taking her up to the third floor, east wing."

Diver and Summer headed to the elevator. "I should have done something," Diver said. "I should have known."

"I was thinking the same thing."

"I can't let anything happen to her, Summer."

"I was thinking that too."

Marquez's room was lit only by a small light over her bed. Beneath the peach blanket, she looked impossibly frail. Her hair fanned over the crisp pillow in dark ribbons.

When they stepped through the door, she closed her eyes. Her lower lip trembled. "I'm sorry," she whispered, and then Diver and Summer ran over and hugged her and yelled at her and cried with her, and then they did it all over again.

"You don't have to walk me down," Summer told Diver as they waited at the elevator half an hour later. "I'm sure I can find the cafeteria. I'll just follow the smell of overcooked cabbage."

"I don't mind. I wanted to talk to you alone. We need to really keep an eye on Marquez, okay? You and me together, I think we can pretty much cover her all the time."

The doors slid open. Diver stepped into the empty elevator, but Summer just stood there, contemplating him.

"What?" Diver demanded, hands upraised.

"Nothing." Summer entered the elevator and jabbed the button for the first floor.

"No, what?"

"It's just . . . I look at you here with Marquez. You practically arm wrestle the night nurse into submission till she agrees you can sleep in Marquez's room. You're ready to turn into the Pill Police to help her. And the way you were just so . . . so *there* for her tonight."

"Is there a problem with that?"

"No. I'm really glad for Marquez. I love her too. She's my best friend, don't forget. It's just that—" She shrugged. She was tired. She shouldn't have started this. She was upset about Marquez and upset about Austin. She most definitely shouldn't have started this. She and Diver had already had this discussion.

The doors opened. Diver stepped into the empty corridor. "It's just that I couldn't be there for Jack and Kim and you back in Minnesota, right?"

Jack and Kim. He could never, ever bring himself to call them Mom and Dad.

"I'm sorry I brought it up. I'm tired, is all. We've done this, Diver. Let's not go through it again."

Summer followed a sign that pointed toward the cafeteria. But Diver persisted, trailing her down the hallway. Other than the occasional nurse or orderly, the hospital seemed deserted. Summer checked her watch. It was so late. She wondered if she should call Seth in California when she got home. It was three hours earlier, but he'd probably be in bed already. Still, it would be nice to hear his voice after this awful night.

"Summer." Diver grabbed her arm, forcing her to a halt. "Jack and Kim are my biological parents. But they were my parents for only two years. I had other parents—" His voice caught. "Bad parents, but still, parents."

"They kidnapped you, Diver. I'd say that rates right up there on the bad-parent scale."

Diver grimaced. "When you found me last summer, it was too much too fast. You pushed so hard. You wanted me to be the brother you'd lost, Jack and Kim wanted me to be the son they'd lost . . . I don't know. I couldn't live up to your expectations." He paused, searching for words. "With Marquez there aren't any expectations. That's why I can be there for her. It's easier."

"That's always the deal with you, Diver. You always do what's easy. You walked out on Mom and Dad without even giving them a chance because it was easy, and now they're divorcing. I'm glad it was easy for you." She choked back tears. "It wasn't so easy for them."

"Please, Summer, whatever there is between

us," Diver said, "whatever bad blood, we need to work together to help Marquez."

"Marquez is my best friend. I'm not the one who needs lessons in loyalty—" She stopped when she saw Blythe and Caroline come through the doors of the cafeteria.

Blythe waved when she saw them. "So? How's she doing?" she asked, walking over.

"She'll be fine," Summer said, trying to collect herself. "She just, uh, overdid it."

"Thank God. Someone needs to slow that girl down a little. Oh, Diver, this is Caroline—"

Caroline gasped. "Oh, my Lord!" she shrieked. "I swear, it really *is* you, isn't it?" She grabbed Diver by the shoulders. "Paul? Paul Lamont? Don't you recognize me?"

Diver shook off her grip and took a step backward. "You've got the wrong guy—"

"Car, this is Diver Smith, Summer's brother," Blythe interjected.

Caroline frowned. "Wow, this is really eerie. I mean, you look *exactly* like this next-door neighbor of mine who—well, never mind, it's a very long story. Are you *sure* you never lived in Virginia? Positively sure?"

Diver offered up one of his patented charming smiles. "I'm sure I'd remember if you'd been my neighbor," he said. "Sorry to disappoint you."

Caroline frowned. "But I—"

"Gotta go," Diver interrupted. With a quick glance at Summer, he headed off down the corridor, practically jogging.

"Boy, I could have sworn that was him," Caroline said. She nudged Summer. "You're absolutely sure he's your brother?"

Summer sighed. "You know, Caroline, sometimes I really wonder."

5

What Diana Wants, Diana Gets

The apartment seemed terribly lonely when Summer got home. The truth was, it wasn't really even "home" yet—she and Diana and Marquez had just moved in a couple of days earlier. And now, with Marquez in the hospital and Diana in California, it felt alien, as if Summer were staying in an empty hotel. A hotel with a really cheesy interior decorator.

After a long search, Summer located Diana's cell phone and dialed Seth. By now she knew the number by heart.

Seth was doing an internship for a company in California that built racing sailboats. He shared an apartment in Newport Beach with some guys from the sailboat company.

Summer wondered if he and Diana had managed to get together that weekend. Diana was in California with her mom, a romance author who was on a book-signing tour. Summer had encouraged Diana to stop in and say hi to Seth if she could find the time. It wasn't nearly as good as visiting Seth herself, of course. But at least she could get the lowdown on Seth's apartment, his roommates, that sort of thing. And more important, she could get a feel for how he was faring without her. It was so hard to read people over the telephone.

The phone rang three times before someone finally picked it up.

"Hello?" The voice was low, throaty, a little annoyed. A girl's voice.

Summer winced. Seth had two guy roommates. This was probably someone's girlfriend. She hoped she wasn't interrupting anything.

"Um, I'm sorry to call so late. Is Seth Warner there?"

A long pause. "Summer?"

"Yes?"

"It's me, Diana."

"Oh, I . . . I didn't recognize your voice. You sounded sleepy."

"Well, it *is* late."

"So you caught up with Seth okay, huh?"

Another pause. "Oh, yes. We had a very interesting evening, actually."

"You want interesting? We've just had the evening from hell here. I came home tonight to find Marquez passed out on the floor—"

"Oh, my God! What happened?"

"She's okay. Just a cut on her head. She's staying overnight at the hospital for observation. But the doctor says she needs some counseling."

"The dieting, right?" Diana sighed. "I already tried to get her to see someone."

"You did?"

"Right before I left for California. She wasn't interested. Damn. I knew she was in trouble."

"Diver thinks we're going to have to keep an eye on her, all of us."

"Yeah." Diana sighed. "Assuming she'll let us." She fell silent.

"Well, um, I guess if you could pass me on to Seth—"

"Seth?" Suddenly Diana's voice was animated. "Yeah, hold on a minute. He's right here."

Summer heard whispered voices, some shuffling, then the sound of someone grabbing the receiver.

"Seth?"

"Yeah, I'm here." The edge in his voice startled Summer. "Where were you tonight, anyway? I called before."

"I—at the hospital. Marquez—"

"Diana just told me. I'm glad Marquez is okay. I meant before that. Where were you before?"

With Austin, Summer answered silently. With Austin, saying good-bye.

Suddenly a terrible thought came to her. What if Diana had told Seth that Austin was living on Coconut Key? Summer had asked her not to mention it. But if it had slipped out accidentally, Seth, being Seth, would no doubt be assuming the worst. . . .

"Seth, what's wrong? You sound kind of weird. Are you upset about something? Is everything okay?"

A short exhalation of breath, then silence.

"Seth?"

"Look, Summer, I'm flying back to Florida with Diana. I've got a little cash saved, and Diana's going to front me the rest till I can pay her back. I've got to see you."

"Oh, Seth, that's so fantastic! I need to see you too, so badly."

"I'm flying back with Diana day after tomorrow, if I can get a flight."

"How long can you stay?"

"I don't know. As long as it takes."

Summer frowned. "What do you mean? Are they giving you time off work this soon? What about the internship?"

"Screw the internship. I just have to see you, okay?"

"Me too. It's like you read my mind. I hate being separated this way. It's so hard."

He didn't answer.

"Seth?"

"Yeah?"

"I love you, Seth."

"Do you?" Seth whispered. "Do you really, Summer?"

"Of course I do," she said. The line hissed with static. "Seth? This is the part where you say 'I love you' back."

"You already know that," Seth said softly, and then the line went dead.

Diana watched Seth as he hung up the phone. His smooth bare chest glistened in the moonlight. He was so beautiful. And so close to being hers completely.

"Are you sure about flying back?" she asked softly. "Maybe you should wait, let things sink in. You're awfully upset right now."

"I'm not ending this over the phone. I want

to see her. I want to hear her tell me to my face that it's over."

Diana began kneading his tight shoulders. "I don't know . . . maybe you're right. Maybe it's better to get this over with quickly. Better for you and for Summer."

"And for you?" he asked caustically.

She let it go. He was angry at her for telling him the truth. It would pass. She could wait. All that mattered was that she was the one in his room at that moment, touching him in the darkness. Not Summer.

"She said she loved me." He said it pleadingly, a question that needed answering.

Diana brushed the nape of his neck with her fingertips. She had to choose her words with care. If she handled this right, Seth would turn to her when he realized it was really over with Summer. But if she pushed too hard, he'd come to see Diana as part of the messy breakup and leave her behind when he left Summer.

"I think Summer probably does love you, Seth, in her way," Diana said carefully.

Seth turned to her. "I have to be sure," he said. "I've got to see her one more time before I . . . you know. Before I end it."

"I know," Diana said. "I understand."

That wasn't what she'd had in mind. She'd

pictured a long-distance breakup, courtesy of AT&T. The usual, with lots of accusations and sobbing and Kleenex. Then Summer would fall into Austin's arms—where she'd spent plenty of time already—and Diana would stick around a while longer to provide Seth with the necessary aid and comfort. By the time his internship was over and he returned to Coconut Key to finish out the summer, they'd all be the best of friends.

Or at least on speaking terms.

Or at least no one would be facing homicide charges.

But if Seth went back to Florida right away, there could be problems. Summer could string him along the way she had the last time, when he'd caught her with Austin. Seth was vulnerable that way. He'd fallen for Summer's promises before.

And then there was the little matter of the engagement ring. That had been a gamble, sure. Diana knew it was only a matter of time before Summer heard about Diana's little ruse.

She'd be furious, of course. First, that Diana had found the missing ring and held on to it. And second, that she'd used it as evidence of Summer's infidelity.

Diana knew what would happen. Summer would explain to Seth how she'd really lost the ring accidentally, and Marquez would back her up. She'd beg Seth to reconsider and give her another chance.

No, the ring maneuver had probably not been one of Diana's smarter moves.

On the other hand, it had gotten her this far. Into Seth's arms.

"Lie down," she whispered. "I'll give you a massage. You're so tense, Seth. You need to relax."

She straddled his waist and ran her hands over his back in slow, deliberate strokes. Her own muscles were as tight as his. She felt anxious and a little guilty.

She could have any guy she wanted. She didn't need these underhanded tricks, this seduction routine. She could look at a guy, crook her finger, and have him running to do her bidding.

Any guy, that is, except Seth.

"Feel better?" she murmured.

"You don't have to do this, Diana."

"I want to."

Maybe it would work out okay after all. They'd fly back, and Seth would see Summer and Austin together, the way Diana had seen them so many times. After all, Austin worked in their building. He would be impossible to avoid. Even if Summer tried to cover up her relationship with him, it would just be a matter of time before Seth caught a shared glimpse, a subtle touch . . . something that would give Summer's true feelings away.

It would be the final nail in the coffin. The end of Summer and Seth.

The beginning of Seth and Diana.

Diana trailed her long nails down Seth's spine. "Seth, I don't think it would be a good idea for you to tell Summer I was the one who told you about Austin."

"Don't you think she'll figure that out on her own, Diana?" Seth said sarcastically.

"All Summer knows right now is that you have a sudden desire to fly home and see her. You'll see for yourself what's going on with her and Austin when you get there. You'll see your ring is no longer on her finger, and that's all you'll need. She doesn't have to know I was the one who started it all."

"What do you care what Summer thinks? I mean, after what we just did . . ."

"You're not sorry, are you?"

"At the moment I don't feel anything, Diana. Except maybe like shoving my fist through the wall."

"She's not worth that kind of anger, Seth.

And as for my caring what Summer thinks . . . look, I don't approve of the way she's treated you or I wouldn't have come to you this way, but I've got to keep living with the girl. I just signed a lease for the summer. Besides, she's my cousin."

Seth rolled over so that she was sitting on his chest. He looked up at her with a smile that threatened to turn into a sneer. "So then you get it all, huh, Diana? No blame, plus me. What a deal."

"I don't get you, Seth, not the way I want. I know you're still in love with Summer. You'll probably always be in love with her."

"Not after this," he said bitterly.

"I know it hurts." Diana combed her fingers through his hair. "I'm so sorry."

Seth stared at her, shaking his head. "I have to tell you, Diana, I just don't see what you get out of this arrangement."

She bent down, brushing her lips against his. "I'm so glad you asked. Allow me to explain."

6

To Sleep, Perchance Not to Dream

*D*iver shifted in the uncomfortable chair beside Marquez's bed. She was sleeping soundly, her mouth open slightly, exhaling in long, slow breaths.

He wished he could be so lucky. All night long he'd been slipping in and out of the same awful dream. Each time he awoke he was bathed in sweat, his heart hammering wildly, his teeth clenched.

He'd had the dream a million times. He knew it by heart, every plot twist, every bizarre turn. Sometimes he even knew it was a dream while he was dreaming.

It should have been reassuring. Like an old TV rerun.

But every single time it was utterly, completely terrifying.

He walked softly to the window and peered through the blinds. No hint of dawn. No reprieve.

He wondered what time it was. Sometimes he actually wished he wore a watch, like normal people. But then, nothing about the life of Diver Smith was normal.

Diver. Jonathan. Paul. Sometimes he wondered what his name really was.

He'd picked up the nickname Diver when he was living on the streets, sleeping on the beach at night and diving under piers to hide from the beach patrol. Before that he'd been Paul, the name his parents—or the people who'd kidnapped him and pretended to be his parents—had called him.

And before then, until the age of two, he'd been Jonathan. That was the name he'd been born with. The name on his birth certificate.

By the time Summer had been born, Jonathan was already just a name in the newspaper, a black-and-white photo on the side of a milk carton. It was the name she'd grown up afraid to say out loud for fear of what it might do to her fragile, desperate parents.

Diver went back to his chair. He was tired, so

tired, but if he closed his eyes, he'd go back to that place he couldn't bear to see, not even in his dreams.

It always started the same way. The playground. The tiny yellow sneakers on his feet. The red ball.

He let his lids fall. He listened to Marquez's steady breathing. In, out, in, out . . . if he concentrated on that soothing sound, maybe he could sleep peacefully, dreamlessly, for once. . . .

But there it was. Cracked, chewed-up red rubber, as if it had been a dog's ball at some point.

Diver knew he would throw the ball. And the part of him watching the dream knew that by throwing the ball he would change his life forever.

It flew. Pretty far, it seemed. It bounced dully on the faded grass. It rolled over to the fence and lay there against the chain link.

A man was standing by the fence. His face was hidden. A woman was in a car nearby, the door open. She was crying, but her face too was hidden.

He ran to get the red ball. He picked it up.

The man reached over the fence to grab him.

He floated, helpless.

In his chair, Diver moaned softly. This was

the part of the dream he dreaded. There would be detours down black highways, lonely houses with echoing corridors, years that blended into years in the space of a dream second.

There would be the funeral, his seven-year-old self in a stiff, too-big suit, the sickly sweet smell of lilies in the air. He would see his mother, his mother who really wasn't his mother, in her peach dress, her face thick with powder. His father would lift him up to the casket, and he would scream.

More detours, more highways, more houses. And then, always and forever, came the fire.

It never hurt in the dream. He walked calmly, feet cool and bare, over sizzling embers. He breathed in the poisonous fumes as though they were crisp mountain air. He could see through the sooty veil of smoke, parting it like a curtain.

And what he saw, every time, was his father, his father who was not his father, lying under a burning support beam. His clothes were ablaze. His hair, even his skin.

He could see his father. He could walk effortlessly through the burning house and touch him. But whenever his father's mouth opened to scream, he could not hear him.

He could not hear him because by that time

Diver was always the one who was screaming.

"Diver, hon, wake up! Diver!"

His eyes flew open.

No smoke. No fire. Marquez was sitting up in bed, rubbing her eyes.

"The dream again?"

Diver nodded. His throat burned. His eyes stung. Sometimes he woke from the dream absolutely certain he was in the middle of a raging inferno.

But of course that fire was over. It had been extinguished long ago.

And so had all record of the boy named Paul.

"Come here," Marquez whispered. She patted the mattress. "Come sleep with me."

Diver stood shakily. He climbed onto the bed and crawled under the sheets. Marquez's body was warm. She felt small against him, breakable.

He should have known she was getting too thin. This was his fault. He didn't know how to take care of people. He couldn't be trusted.

He was crying. He hadn't cried like this in a long time, perhaps years. Maybe not even since the fire.

Marquez took his hand. "It's okay. You're with me now. It was just a dream, Diver. It wasn't real."

But it was real. He couldn't tell Marquez that. He couldn't tell anyone, ever.

Because if they found him, it would be the end.

He ran his fingers over the scar on his hip, the flesh hard and rubbery where the burn had healed badly.

When Marquez had asked about it, he'd told her he'd tipped over a pot of boiling water on the stove as a little kid. She'd laughed and said, "I bet you were a handful. I bet you were a beautiful kid. Don't you have any pictures?"

"No pictures," he'd told her. "My parents weren't exactly the sentimental type."

After a long while he stopped crying. Marquez was asleep again, breathing in, out, in, out, slowly and steadily. He lay beside her and watched her breathe until the first pale hints of dawn appeared.

7

Summer Is Definitely Not a Morning Person

The midmorning sun poured through Summer's bedroom window, painting the walls a brilliant gold. She squinted, then burrowed beneath her blanket.

She'd had a lousy night's sleep, filled with unsettling dreams. She didn't remember them, not exactly. But she knew Seth and Austin had been featured stars. It was probably just as well that she couldn't recall the details.

Summer forced her eyes open. Even with the flowered sheet over the window, the light was blinding. Maybe she should think about getting real curtains.

Florida light. Nothing like the milky Minnesota sunlight she'd grown up with. This was go-to-the-beach-and-bake sun. It made you want to grab your sexiest bathing suit, your darkest shades, and the trashiest novel you wouldn't mind being seen with in public and head for the ocean. . . .

Reality check.

None of that was on the agenda that day. Her first priority was getting Marquez home from the hospital and giving her a nice lecture on the Five Basic Food Groups and Why We Must Eat Them.

Following that, if there was time, Summer needed to hit the streets and do some more job-hunting. She was getting increasingly desperate. Most of the good waitress jobs were taken, and waiting tables was her only marketable skill—unless you counted the fact that she typed about eleven words per minute, only slightly faster than an untrained chimp.

She climbed out of bed, shielding her eyes from the glare. A glance in her mirror made her shudder. She had major morning hair.

Should she call the hospital, she wondered, or would Marquez call her? The doctor might even have released her already.

Summer turned on the radio. Soul Asylum. Excellent bed-making music. The least she could do was have the apartment nice and neat for Marquez's return. Marquez had been on a real cleaning jag lately. Very un-Marquez-like, and a little disturbing, actually, since she'd always been so messy that she made Summer feel organized.

Diana's side of the room was already clean. Her bed was crisply made, her side of the closet neat. Her still-unpacked boxes were piled in tall stacks against the wall. One box was out of place—old letters, it looked like. Summer shoved it into the closet. She glanced at a postcard of Paris from Diana's mother. It surprised Summer a little that her cousin saved things like that. On the surface, at least, she wasn't exactly the most sentimental person. But even Diana probably had a softer side.

Diana would return the next day, and with her, Seth. He'd sounded so strange on the phone the night before, so distant. Summer knew she should have been thrilled he was coming back for a visit, even a short one. But she couldn't help feeling uneasy.

One way or another, Seth was going to find out that Austin was living on Coconut Key. With Austin working downstairs at Jitters, it was just a matter of time. That would lead to a lot of pointed questions, along the lines of "Why the hell didn't you tell me this?"

Add to that the fact that she'd reapplied to Carlson College, right there on Coconut Key. If she was accepted again, it would call into question all the plans Seth and she had made: going to the University of Wisconsin together, spending all four years there together, then getting married . . .

Her hand flew to her mouth. She'd almost forgotten.

She touched the bare spot where her engagement ring should have been. She could *feel* its absence, a phantom sensation, the way they said you could still feel a missing limb long after it was gone.

What would she tell Seth about the ring? "It could have happened to anyone, Seth. I was just painting the apartment, and I took it off and put it on the windowsill so I wouldn't get paint on it, and then it just sort of vanished. . . ."

Seth would never understand. He would never understand because if he'd been wearing the ring, he would never in a million years have taken it off.

Of course, she thought with sudden bitterness, guys didn't even wear engagement rings. Only girls. What was that all about? How come girls were the ones stuck with the awesome responsibility?

It was too much . . . Austin, college, the ring. Seth would never forgive her for her many and assorted sins.

Well, that was one more chore to add to the day's list. By the end of the day, she had to find a perfect replica of her engagement ring. Preferably one under ten bucks.

After a cup of hot tea, Summer called the hospital. Marquez had already been discharged. Summer hoped she was coming straight home to rest up. But knowing Marquez, she would probably head directly to Jitters to work a double shift, then throw in a triathlon for good measure.

Diver had been right about that, at least. They were going to have to keep a close eye on Marquez. Very close.

Someone knocked softly on the door. Summer ran to get it, thinking it was Diver and Marquez. She'd swung the door wide open before she realized it wasn't Marquez at all.

"Austin."

He was carrying a bouquet of yellow daisies. His eyes were bloodshot. His hair was tangled. He needed a shave.

Obviously he hadn't slept well either.

"Thought you were rid of me, I know.

May I?" He stepped inside before she could answer.

"They're very pretty," Summer said with a nod at the flowers, "but I can't take them, Austin."

"Good thing. They're not for you." Austin tossed the bouquet on the kitchen counter. "They're for Marquez. Blythe told me what happened when I got in for the morning shift today. I went out and bought them on my break."

"That was very thoughtful. I'll be sure to see she gets them." Summer started to fill a glass of water for the flowers, then rolled her eyes. "God, I just realized I look like crap."

"Day-old crap," Austin amended. "But so do I." He shrugged. "Breaking up is hard to do."

Summer ran to her bedroom to put on a robe. When she returned to the living room, Austin was on the back balcony, gazing down at the sparkling pool. Or at Caroline, who was stretched out on a lounge chair, glistening with suntan oil.

"Heartbroken, you say?" Summer asked wryly.

He turned to her. Gently he combed her tangled hair with his fingers. "Completely," he whispered.

Deep inside her something stirred. She closed her eyes and took a step back.

"Austin, I think you should go. It's too hard . . . I can't keep seeing you this way. We need to make a clean break." She tightened the belt of her robe. "The thing is, Seth is flying back here tomorrow for a visit, and, well . . ."

Instead of getting angry, Austin just shook his head. He almost looked amused. "You'd like me to keep a low profile, is that it? Maybe just disappear from the scene entirely? I hear Canada's nice this time of year."

"I only meant—"

"I know what you meant, Summer. You want me to make it easy on you—"

He was interrupted by a knock at the door. "That's probably Marquez," Summer said, running for the door. "She doesn't have her keys."

Marquez practically flew into the room, followed by Diver. "Home, sweet home!" she cried. "Man, I have *got* to take another shower. I still reek of hospital."

Summer gave her a long hug. "You look good. How do you feel?"

"Scarred for life." Marquez pushed back her hair to reveal a small Band-Aid on her forehead. "My brilliant modeling career is over before it started. Whoa, flowers?" She grabbed the bouquet and inhaled deeply. "You shouldn't have."

"I didn't. I mean, I was going to, but I sort of overslept. They're from Austin. He's out on the porch."

"What a sweetheart."

"Not really." Austin came in and gave Marquez a kiss on the cheek. "I have ulterior motives. I'm hoping to pick up some of your shifts."

"No way." Marquez laughed. "I am back on active duty as of tonight."

"Marquez," Diver said sternly, "the doctor said to take it easy."

She rolled her eyes. "Okay, okay. You can have my dinner shift tonight, Austin. But that's it. I'm broke. When I get that hospital bill, I will be beyond broke."

Diver wrapped his arm around her protectively. "I told you I'll help with that. I'm a wealthy man now."

"You're a less destitute man," Marquez corrected.

"I got that job at the new wildlife rehab center," Diver explained. "Called them this morning, and they were ready to put me to work yesterday."

Summer frowned. With Diver working close by, she was going to be forced to see even more of him. "Congratulations," she said neutrally.

"I need to find a place in town as soon as I can."

Marquez nudged him. "I told him we wouldn't mind a male roommate for a while, right, Summer?"

Summer shrugged. "Sure. I guess. You should check with Diana first, though. She'll be home tomorrow. With Seth."

"I believe that's my exit cue," Austin said. He winked at Marquez. "Glad you're okay, kid." He opened the door, then hesitated. "Hey, Diver, a brilliant thought just occurred to me. If you're stuck, you could always double up with me at my place. It's the size of a postage stamp, but the roaches are the size of poodles. So it sort of evens out."

"That'd be great, Austin," Diver said. He cast a sidelong glance at Summer. "Easier than staying here."

"Yeah, at my place you can belch to your heart's content and scratch yourself with impunity." Austin grinned. "Chicks don't approve of that kind of thing."

"Chicks don't approve of saying 'chicks,' either," Marquez said, giving him a playful sock in the arm.

"Stop by anytime, Diver," Austin said.

"How about tomorrow afternoon?" Diver asked. "That'll give me time to get my stuff together."

"Great. It's over on Palm Avenue." Austin gave Summer a wistful smile. "Ask Summer. She knows just where it is."

8

Look Who's Not Talking

I told you we should have come to Woolworth first!" Marquez held her discovery high. "*Voilà!* I give you the Hope Diamond!"

Summer examined the ring in its little black velvet box. "More like hopeless."

"The price is right. Seven ninety-five."

"This is never going to work, is it?"

"Summer, we have been to every jewelry store and drugstore and antique store on the key. Where else can we go?"

"Crappy Fake Diamonds R Us?" Summer examined the ring carefully. "You know, it *does* look an awful lot like the one Seth gave me."

"You don't suppose . . . ?" Marquez grinned.

"He always was kind of cheap with a buck. Buy it, Summer. Seth's coming tomorrow. This is as good as it's gonna get."

"I'm sorry. Am I wearing you out? Diver was right. You should have stayed home and rested this afternoon."

"I am not an invalid, Summer," Marquez nearly shouted. If Summer said one more sweet, solicitous thing to her, she was going to scream. "Although you'll be one soon if you don't shut up."

"The doctor said—"

"I fainted. I overdid it a little. Okay? Since when is it a federal crime to try to lose a little weight?"

Summer snapped her mouth shut, but Marquez could practically see the words fighting to escape from her tightly pressed lips.

"Diver has already given me the lecture, Summer. You're off the hook."

Summer examined another ring, pouting.

"I know the drill, okay? Eat my veggies. Exercise in moderation. Stop counting calories. I'm beautiful, I'm perfect, I'm already too skinny, I'm the Cuban-American Kate Moss."

Summer just looked at her, worry written all over her face. Marquez's own mother had never looked at her with that much concern.

60

"Oh, all right, go ahead, get it over with," Marquez groaned. "I can see you're going to explode otherwise."

"It's just that you really had us scared, Marquez. I mean, it's easy for *you* to crack jokes." Summer's lower lip trembled. "*I'm* the one who found you lying there. I'm the one who thought you were . . . you know . . ." Summer sniffled. "And all I could think of was that if anything happened to you—"

"You'd get to have my bedroom?"

Summer sniffled louder.

"What, then? My stereo? My car?"

"It's not funny, Marquez."

"You're as bad as Diver. He was all weepy too. Jeez, one little teeny fainting spell. Is your whole family this emotional?"

Summer wasn't smiling. "Okay," Marquez relented, "I promise I'll be good, okay? Really, I promise."

"And you'll go to that counseling group?"

"You are going to make someone a really obnoxious mother someday. You will be the mother of all mothers."

"Marquez."

"I don't see what good it'll do. They'll all be sitting in a circle having . . . you know, *feelings*."

"It won't kill you to try it, Marquez."

"There may be hugging involved."

Summer wasn't budging.

"God, all right. One time. And in return you promise to shut up about this?"

"I promise." Summer was beaming. "One more thing. I told Diver I'd be sure you had lunch."

"Sure, fine. Whatever."

"And one more thing."

"Do you understand the phrase 'pushing your luck'?"

Summer hesitated. "The doctor asked if maybe you'd been taking something."

"Something?" Marquez echoed sarcastically.

"Um, pills. You know." Summer looked embarrassed in that sweet midwestern way she had.

"Diver already asked me that, Summer. The answer's no. I mean, please."

"Okay." Summer didn't look entirely convinced.

Marquez took a deep breath. She couldn't take all this nosing into her life. She felt as though she were suffocating. They didn't understand that she had it under control. But the more they poked at her, the less control she'd have.

Still, if she fought too hard, they'd be all over

her even worse than they were already. Between Diver and Summer, she'd feel as though she had a twenty-four-hour guard.

Better to humor them. Get them off her case.

"Buy the ring, then we'll eat something," she said wearily. "I'll be outside. I need some air."

"You're okay?" Summer's hand was on her shoulder.

Marquez shook it off. "I just need some air. That's all. Just some air."

"This isn't exactly what I had in mind when I said lunch," Summer said half an hour later as they sat down on the beach.

"Chili dogs?" Marquez plucked off a piece of bun. "It's classic beach food. Besides, I had a craving."

"Well, that's a good sign, I guess."

They stretched out on the fine white sand, letting the waves tease their bare feet. It was late afternoon, and the crowds had thinned to a few die-hard sunbathers and some surfers trying to ride the halfhearted waves. The air still shimmered with heat. The sky was a pale, washed-out blue.

"I wish we had our suits on," Summer said.

"Speak for yourself," Marquez replied. She was wearing a pair of long, baggy shorts and one of Diver's big T-shirts, but even in her camouflage clothes she knew she looked like a beached whale. She cast a glance at Summer, who had on a crop top and khaki shorts. She was one of those naturally, unfairly thin girls who could eat anything without gaining an ounce. Summer was irrefutable evidence that life was not fair.

"So," Summer said, changing the subject, "you think Seth will believe the ring?" She held out her hand, displaying the little pretend diamond. "I wish it fit better. It's kind of big."

"Tell Seth you lost weight." Marquez shook her head. "I don't get why you don't just admit to him that you lost it."

"I will. If I don't find it, I will. But it's only been a few days, and it could still turn up in the apartment somewhere." Summer took a bite of her chili dog, then wiped her mouth with the back of her hand. "And you know Seth. He's so sensitive. He'll think it means something, my losing the ring. Besides, he and I will have enough to discuss."

"Austin, you mean."

Summer lay back on the sand with a sigh. "Austin."

Marquez watched a seagull bobbing on the

waves. Once again she tried to remember the phone call the previous night. Seth had called, she was pretty sure of that. She'd been exercising. She'd been a little out of it, winded, fuzzy. He'd asked her . . . at least she *thought* he'd asked her . . . if Summer was with Austin.

What had she told him? Had she told him the truth?

Why couldn't she remember? Was it the pills? Maybe it was because she'd hit her head so hard.

Why would she have told him the truth? It wasn't Marquez's style to butt in where she didn't belong. She would have said something vague, some half-truth, wouldn't she?

"Yeah, Seth. She's with Austin." She could almost hear herself saying it.

Marquez glanced at Summer. Her eyes were closed.

Quickly Marquez tore off a hunk of her chili dog and buried it in the sand. Some seagull was going to dine well that night.

"Summer, why do you think Seth is coming back?" Marquez asked. "His internship's for another month, right? And it must cost a fortune to get a ticket on short notice."

"He said Diana was fronting him some money." Summer rolled onto her side. "I'll tell you the truth. He sounded funny on the phone. Sort of . . . cold."

"You don't suppose Diana told him about Austin?"

"I asked her not to. But you know, it's not like there's anything to tell, really. I told Austin I want him out of my life. And I can't help it if he chooses to live in the same town I live in."

"Still, it's not like you mentioned it to Seth. He'll be freaked when he finds out. After all, you fell for Austin over spring break."

"I know. I blew it. I was just trying to keep things simple, and the more I tried, the more complicated things got. I should have told Seth the truth right from the start."

"Hey, everything will be fine. That ring could easily pass for one costing twice as much." Marquez laughed. "Which is to say fifteen bucks and some change."

"Too bad I don't have a job. Maybe I could have afforded a better fake stone. Oh, well. I've got another interview coming up."

"As what?"

"As . . ." Summer hesitated. "As, um, a companion."

"Dogs are companions, Summer. Being a companion is not a job for a person."

Summer tossed some sand on Marquez's leg.

"It involves running errands for some nice young guy who's recovering from a car accident. At least I hope he's nice. I'm just about out of job options."

"There's always Jitters."

"Not with Austin there."

"What about that clerk job at Flipper for Freaks?"

"The Dolphin Interactive Therapy Institute," Summer corrected. "They never called me back. Could be they noticed I can't type, take dictation, or operate a copy machine. Or make coffee without a recipe book."

"How about your sunny disposition? Besides, I'll bet that with intensive training you could master the coffee."

"It's probably just as well. That's sort of Diana's thing. She's been volunteering there a long time, and you know how she is. She has her own private world she doesn't want anyone intruding on."

Marquez sneaked another wad of chili dog under the sand. "Diana and volunteering. It's hard to say those words in the same breath. It's like *Satan* and *bake sale*. It just doesn't quite work."

"I think Diana has a sweeter side we just don't get to see."

"Visible only with the aid of an electron microscope."

Summer laughed. "Like there's this box of letters she's got in our room. Did you see it? Full of old stuff, postcards from my aunt Mallory, that sort of thing. Would you ever in a million years have dreamed Diana would save letters from her mother?"

Marquez blinked. Letters. The box of letters. She'd dropped it when she was cleaning up Diana's room. The letters had scattered all over. When she was picking them up, she'd seen it—a letter from Diana to Seth, never sent. A love letter.

"Marquez? You okay?"

"Yeah. I've just got sun-stun."

"Me too."

She could tell Summer. Maybe it was her duty. If Diana and Seth had been together over New Year's . . .

If Diana was still in love with Seth . . .

If Marquez had told Seth that Summer and Austin were together the night before . . .

If, if, if. Her head was spinning. What if she was wrong? She hated getting involved in other people's messes. She hated the way people poked into hers.

It was perfectly possible that Seth would show up the next day and everything would be fine. Besides, if Marquez needed to confront anyone about all this, it was probably Diana.

Now *there* was a happy thought.

She shoved the last of her chili dog under the sand.

"I'm stuffed," Summer said.

"Me too."

"I'm glad you ate. I feel like I did my duty."

"Mission accomplished," Marquez said softly. She smoothed the sand with her hand.

She'd wait and see what happened with Summer and Seth. Sometimes the best thing to do was just bury your problems.

9

Diamonds Aren't Forever

Through the plane window Diana watched the familiar line of islands unfurl, a string of green pearls in a blindingly bright blue ocean. It was a sight that always comforted her, but that day she was too jumpy to care.

She laced her fingers through Seth's. He didn't react, didn't tighten his grip. But he didn't pull away either. He was in neutral, noncommittal. He'd been that way since talking to Summer.

She knew the signs. She'd pulled the same act with far too many guys—being cool, unreachable. Seth was holding back, and it made her angry. But she couldn't push. She would just have to watch this movie unfold and hope it had a happy ending. For her, anyway.

"Seth?"

He looked at her, not quite smiling.

"What are you going to say when you see Summer?"

He pulled his hand away. "I'm really not sure, Diana. I guess I'll just give her a chance to tell me her side of the story."

Her side. That was not a good sign. It meant he was weakening. It meant he wanted to find a way to forgive Summer.

"What could she possibly say in her defense?"

"I don't know," Seth snapped. "I just want—" He looked away. "I want to know that she really doesn't love me anymore. I want to hear it."

Again Diana took his hand. She could say it now. The way she'd tried to say it in her letters. It wouldn't be so hard just to whisper the words, would it? "I love you, Seth." Would that be so hard?

"I—" The rest got caught in her throat.

"What?"

"I just wanted to say I'm glad I can be here for you. And I'm glad we had the last couple of days together. It was good, wasn't it?"

He gave a terse nod.

"Don't let yourself get hurt any more, Seth.

Just remember that you've been through this before with Summer. She already told you once it was over with Austin. You can't trust her."

This time Seth squeezed her hand. He held on so tightly that it hurt, but at least it was something.

In her mind she tried out the words again.

I love you, Seth.

She wondered if she'd ever have the nerve to say it out loud.

Seth saw her lying there by the side of the pool, asleep. She had on the two-piece bathing suit she'd bought for spring break, the one he'd helped her pick out. He'd sneaked into the dressing room and stolen a glance over the door, then a kiss.

Seth walked along the cement pathway toward the sparkling blue-tiled pool. No one else was around, although he had a sneaking suspicion that Diana and Marquez were spying on him from the third-floor balcony.

Summer's body glistened with oil. Her hair, spilling over the side of the lounge chair, caught the late afternoon sun like spun gold.

He paused and wiped his brow. It was humid in southern Florida, much hotter than in California. Already he'd forgotten what summer heat in the Keys was like.

He tried to summon up the rage he'd felt for the past two days. The feeling of betrayal—gutwrenching, absolute betrayal—he'd felt when Diana had shown him the photo of Summer and Austin. Worse still, the emotion he'd felt at the moment when she'd shown him Summer's ring.

He'd shopped every jewelry store in Eau Claire before deciding on that ring. It wasn't the fanciest or anywhere near the biggest. But it had seemed to him, when he'd found it in the little jewelry store downtown, to be perfectly Summer. Simple, sparkling, clear, honest.

He had known instantly that it was the diamond that belonged on her finger.

It had cost a hell of a lot more than he'd planned on. He'd worked double shifts at Subway, shoveled mountains of snow, even picked up a paper route from a friend.

But it had been worth it just to see the expression on her beautiful face that night at the prom.

If he closed his eyes, he could see Diana's hand holding the ring, the symbol of his vanity and stupidity. How could he ever have believed Summer would be his forever? How could he have been fool enough to trust her after the way she'd betrayed him with Austin over spring break?

Another picture came unbidden to him: a

picture of Diana, hair tangled, face flushed, lips swollen from his kisses.

But that was not what this was about.

This was about Summer and *her* betrayal.

This was about the ring she no longer wore.

He was only inches from her now. To his annoyance, his eyes filled with tears. He looked weak, coming back to Florida. He was signaling that he wasn't ready to give her up, and already that was revealing way too much.

He knelt beside her. How many times had he kissed those lips? Even in his anger he wanted to kiss her again. Just one more time.

She stirred. Her eyes opened.

"Seth?" she whispered.

She sat up and put her arms around his neck. She smelled of coconut oil. Her skin was hot and damp.

She was going to kiss him, but he couldn't let that happen. If she did, he might forget why he was there and who was right and who was wrong.

He grabbed her hands to push her away.

And then he felt it. On her finger, where it belonged.

His ring.

10

Black Widows and Avenging Angels

S it," Marquez commanded.

With a deep sigh Diana dropped into a chair at a window table. Jitters was quiet, with just a few customers sipping lattes while they read the afternoon paper. The front door was wide open, allowing in the humid air along with a host of flies. The tall palms lining the cobblestone street cast long shadows, shrouding the window in shade.

Marquez took a chair across from her. Her arms were folded over her chest. Her dark eyes were narrow slits. She looked like a simmering pot in serious danger of boiling over.

No matter. Diana was about to go nuclear herself.

Just a few minutes earlier Seth had kissed Summer. Diana had seen it with her own prying eyes.

After all he knew, how could he *kiss* Summer?

Diana stared out the window. Two lifeguards in red beach patrol swim trunks passed by, probably heading home for the day. A few steps behind them was a young couple. The guy was toting a beach umbrella and a cooler. The girl had her hand on his bare back. She stood on tiptoe to whisper something in his ear.

Diana thought of Seth, of the way his tight, muscular back had felt beneath her hands. The way his mouth had felt, skimming kisses along her neck.

She shook off the thought and turned back to Marquez. "So what is it you want to talk about?" she demanded. "Is there some reason we couldn't have done this upstairs in the privacy of our own apartment? I mean, I just got home, Marquez."

"We can't do this in the privacy of our own apartment because when we were up there you insisted on hanging over the balcony so you could eavesdrop on Summer and Seth."

"She was kissing him."

"In case you've forgotten, they're engaged."

"In case you've forgotten," Diana shot back, "Summer's been getting hot and heavy with Austin ever since Seth went to California—" She stopped herself. She was nearly shouting, and Blythe was on her way over to take their order.

"Hey, guys. Back already, Diana? How was California?"

"Like Florida, only three hours earlier."

"Seth came back to see Summer," Marquez added.

"Cool. I'm anxious to meet the love of her life."

Diana rolled her eyes. "I'll have an iced coffee, Blythe. And one of those low-fat muffins."

"Marquez?" Blythe asked.

Marquez shook her head. "I already ate."

"It's on me," Diana said, softening her tone a little.

"No, thank you," Marquez said pointedly.

"How's your head, by the way?" Blythe asked. "You really had us scared the other night."

"Just a couple of stitches, no biggie."

"Sure you don't want a muffin? If I had your figure, I'd be scarfing 'em by the ton."

"Really, Blythe, I'm fine."

Diana waited till Blythe was gone, then said,

"I'm sorry about what happened to you, Marquez."

"And oh, by the way, you told me so, right?"

"No, actually, I wasn't thinking that at all."

Marquez rolled her eyes. "One one thousand, two one thousand—"

"What exactly are you doing, Marquez?"

"Counting the moments until you give me The Lecture. You know, the one I've already had from Diver and Summer about taking care of myself. How water isn't one of the five basic food groups, et cetera, et cetera, blah, blah, blah. That lecture."

Diana smiled gently. "No. No lecture." She saw the challenge in Marquez's eyes: I dare you to try to fix me. I dare you to take away my pain.

Diana had been there herself the previous summer, and for a long time before that. Maybe it hadn't been exactly the same pain, but she'd been stuck in a depression so dark it had threatened to take her down with it.

"I don't want to nag you and I'm not going to lecture you. But I do want to tell you that I've been . . . mixed up . . . before. And sometimes it helps to talk to someone who can be objective."

"No way."

"I didn't want to either. But there were some

people at the Dolphin Institute who worked with the kids there. Counselors. And they helped me get through the stuff with Adam and Ross."

"Diana, *you* were nearly raped by your boyfriend's brother. *I,* on the other hand, got a little dizzy. I fail to see the comparison."

Diana tapped her fingers on the table. She was tempted to give up, but she knew that was just what Marquez wanted.

"I know you're strapped for cash right now," Diana said. "I'd really like to help you out with the counseling costs. It'd sort of be . . . you know, like things coming full circle."

"I am not interested in becoming your pet project. And no way am I taking any more of your damn money!" Marquez exploded, so loudly that customers looked up in alarm.

Diana held up her hands as if she were placating an onrushing bull. She couldn't handle Marquez's legendary temper just then. It wasn't the time or place. Later on she'd try again.

"All right, all right, whatever. If you don't want my help, though, keep in mind there are places that will do the counseling for free, or—"

Marquez pounded her fist on the table. "We are not here to discuss my battle with cellulite. We are here to discuss you. *You,* Diana. Predatory witch of the planet."

Blythe returned with Diana's coffee and muffin. "Listen, I wanted to ask you guys something, but I'm getting the feeling this isn't a good time. Am I right?"

"Yes," Marquez growled.

"No," Diana said. "What is it, Blythe?"

"I just wanted to tell you that I'm having a little party this evening. I get off in fifteen minutes, then I'm heading over to Turtle Beach to do a barbecue. It's sort of for Caroline, this friend of mine who's visiting. And, well, I know you just got back, Diana, and Summer will probably be busy with Seth, but it'd be great if you could stop by."

"Thanks, Blythe," Diana said politely. She kept her gaze trained on Marquez as if she were an attack dog who might pounce if Diana let down her guard. "I'll pass the word."

"Great." Blythe grinned. "Now I'll let you get back to your argument."

"It's not an argument," Diana said.

Marquez nodded. "It's more like a nuclear skirmish."

"You don't have to tell me about it. Why do you think I don't have any roommates?"

Diana leaned across the table when Blythe was out of earshot. "Excuse me? Did I hear you right? Predatory witch of the planet?"

"Good point. I should have said universe."

"I'm impressed, Marquez." Diana took a sip from her coffee. "*Predatory* is a certified four-syllable word. Too bad you have no idea what it means."

"Oh, I looked it up, Diana." Marquez checked the door and lowered her voice. "It said 'See New Year's Eve.'"

Diana did not allow herself to react. She kept her expression carefully neutral. She took another sip of her coffee. She tore off a bit of her muffin.

On the outside she looked unfazed. Inside was another story. Her stomach was busily trying out for the Olympic gymnastics team.

How did Marquez know? How could she possibly *know*?

"I don't know what you're talking about, Marquez," she said, her voice as smooth as silk.

"I found the letter, Diana. The love letter you never sent to Seth. I know you're still in love with him. And it doesn't take a rocket scientist to figure out why you went out to California."

"And why is that?"

Marquez favored Diana with an arctic smile. "I'll give you a clue. It wasn't to spend quality time with mommy dearest."

For a fraction of a second Diana wanted to bolt. Run away, lick her wounds, regroup.

She was furious with Marquez for going through her private letters. She was horrified at the potential consequences if all this came out.

But mostly she was desperately humiliated to have been found out this way. Especially by Marquez, of all people.

Tears stung her eyes, which just added to the embarrassment. She looked away, biting down on her lower lip to keep it from quivering.

"Okay," Diana said at last. "So you know. Now what?"

"Now you tell me," Marquez said darkly, "how you could pull a thing like this with your own cousin. Summer is a stand-up girl, Diana. How could you do this to her? To me, sure. I could handle it—"

"Unfortunately, your taste runs toward guys with parole officers, Marquez."

"Not Diver," Marquez said proudly.

"Okay, he's the exception that proves the rule." Diana sneaked a quick dab at her eyes with her napkin. "Look, I know how this seems. But before you accuse me of any more mortal sins, you should remember this, Marquez. I tried like crazy to get Summer and Seth back together over spring break. I was the one who went to Seth and said, 'Look, you've made your share of mistakes, too, Seth. Give her a second chance.'" She took a shaky breath. "So he did, and what did he get for his trouble? Austin Reed, right back in the picture. You can say what you want, Marquez. But Summer's still in love with Austin. I'm sorry. I think Seth deserves better than that."

"So instead of Summer he gets Vampira, Queen of the Undead?"

"Instead of Summer," Diana whispered, "he gets someone who really loves him."

For the first time Marquez seemed to relent. She leaned back in her chair, toying with a package of Sweet'n Low, lost in thought. "I'll give you this much. It's true that Summer's real confused right now. I think she has strong feelings for Seth and for Austin. But she told Austin it was over, Diana. I think she's worried sick about losing Seth." She gave a laugh. "I mean, we spent an entire day searching for a fake ring to replace her engagement ring."

Diana swallowed. "You did?" she asked, attempting nonchalance. "And did you find something?"

"Oh, yeah. It's a pretty convincing fake too. Turns out Seth could have spent seven ninety-five and saved himself a fortune."

She should never have taken that ring to California. She should have known that ruse would come back to haunt her.

She was such an idiot.

But she'd been desperate. And desperate times called for desperate measures.

"This just proves my point," Diana said, embarrassed by the plaintive sound of her own voice. "This is just the kind of unfair tactic Summer pulls. Why not just tell Seth she lost the ring? If there's nothing there, why not just tell him about Austin?"

"Because it would hurt Seth, Diana. Because she wants to protect him. I know that's a difficult concept for you to grasp, since you're a great believer in the black widow approach to mating. But that's how Summer is. I'm not saying she's not making a mess in the process, but her heart's in the right place."

Diana looked out the window, watching the shadows shift with the breeze. "So now what? Now you're going to tell her everything?"

Marquez dropped her head into her hands. "I don't know," she said wearily. "I don't know what the hell to do. I hate soap operas. I watch Dan Rather, not *Days of Our Lives*. I don't know—you tell me."

"You're going to follow *my* advice?"

"No, I'm going to do the opposite of whatever you tell me to do."

"Marquez, I won't deny I'd hoped Seth would choose me over Summer. But if that's not the way it's going to work out, what good will it do for you to tell her the truth? If Summer finds out about Seth and me, it'll be over between them for sure."

Marquez lifted her head. "Yeah, but if I don't tell her, evil will go unpunished. I can't let you just walk away from this, Diana."

"So all of a sudden you're the FBI?"

"I like to think of myself as God's avenging angel."

Diana crumpled up her napkin and tossed it aside. "I'll be punished, all right." Tears came again, and this time she let them fall. "I won't get Seth."

Marquez nodded. "For once, Diana, it appears you are actually telling the truth. Which worries me, since I believe that's one of the first signs of the apocalypse."

"Well, then, I'm glad we cleared the air." Diana shoved back her chair. "Just one more thing. If you ever go prying into my personal life again, you will be very, very sorry."

"I was just cleaning up your mess, Diana. The box of letters slipped."

"And you accidentally pulled that particular letter out of its envelope and accidentally read it. What are the odds of that, I wonder?"

"It was a real fluke," Marquez agreed.

Diana didn't smile. "You betrayed our friendship, Marquez."

"What friendship? We can't have one, not after the way you betrayed Summer."

"Fine. You won't see me grieving." Diana dropped a five-dollar bill on the table and walked away without another word.

Halfway upstairs Diana changed her mind. She headed outside and around the house, toward the backyard.

She should never have written that letter. Wasn't that the unwritten lesson of politicians? Shred all the evidence. Deniability was everything.

She paused behind a stand of palm trees. Summer and Seth were still by the pool, deep in conversation. His hand was on her thigh, and he was gazing at her like a worshipful puppy. It was a miracle his tongue wasn't hanging out.

Diana had given him so much. She thought of their weekend together. His warm sheets. The dark night falling over them like a secret.

She'd shown him her heart.

She'd done that only once before, with Adam. He had betrayed her. It had taken her a long time to find a way to get even with him, but she had.

If Seth was just using her, if he was going to crawl back into Summer's arms, then Diana had nothing more to lose. Her self-respect would already be in tatters.

This time she already knew how she'd fight back.

That letter might come in handy after all.

11

She's Not Gonna Wash That Man Right Out of Her Hair

When Diana returned to the apartment, she found Marquez in the kitchen doing dishes.

"Oh. It's just you," Marquez snarled.

"I'm taking a shower."

"By all means, keep me posted."

Diana made a beeline for the bathroom. She cranked up Marquez's portable radio, which sat on the orange crate that served as a makeshift table. Joan Osborne was wailing bitterly about lost love. Perfect shower music for the newly betrayed.

She gazed at her reflection. What was it about Summer that Seth found so irresistible? Or maybe the question was, what was it about Diana that he found so resistible?

Or maybe the question was, how could she have made such a mess of things?

Diana stripped off her clothes, turned the shower on as hot as she could stand it, and stepped under the spray. She wanted to wash off the hours of travel dirt she'd accumulated. And, if possible, she wanted to wash away the residue of ickiness she felt about Seth and her. It was equal parts guilt, distaste, and anger. She doubted a little Dial lather and hot water could remove it.

Diana surveyed the assortment of shampoos perched on the edge of the tub. It was amazing how much stuff in plastic bottles accumulated when you gave three girls one shower to share. Marquez was all Suave products, no frills. Summer bought anything that smelled good. Diana bought her shampoo and conditioner from salons, and the bottles always had pretend words such as *volumizing* on the label.

She selected something from the Body Shop that smelled like tangerines. It belonged to Summer. Swiping it was not as gratifying as Diana had hoped. It did not exactly make up for the awful poolside kiss she'd witnessed.

Someone knocked at the door.

"I'm in the shower, Marquez," she called.

The door opened a crack. "It's not Marquez. It's me, Seth. Can I come in?"

Diana peered around the shower curtain. "Is Summer coming too?" she inquired coldly.

"She's down in the laundry room. And Marquez is checking the mail." Seth glanced over his shoulder. "We have to talk, Diana. Now."

Diana motioned him in. "If Summer finds you in here, Seth, you're the one who gets to explain why we're suddenly into group showers."

Seth slipped in and leaned against the door. He crossed his arms over his chest. "She's wearing my ring," he reported in a low, ominous voice.

Diana rinsed off her hair. She turned off the shower and held out her hand. "Gimme a towel, at least."

"Sure. As soon as you give me an explanation."

"Seth, I'm wet and naked and not in the mood for an inquisition. The ring's a fake, obviously."

Seth passed her a towel, careful to lower his eyes.

"What, all of a sudden you're not interested?" Diana demanded. "As I recall it, you were plenty interested the other night."

She wrapped the towel around her and stepped out of the shower. She felt slightly ridiculous and extremely self-conscious.

Seth was staring at his hazy reflection. "A fake," he repeated, watching himself say the word, as if he could locate the truth in the mirror.

"She bought a cheap ring to fake you out when she found out you were coming home. Marquez told me."

Seth stared at her. He had the tortured look of a math student tackling an unsolvable problem. "But why would she do that?" he asked in a whisper.

"How do I know? I've long since given up reading Summer's complicated little mind. She may seem like sweetness and light, Seth, but she's manipulating you all over the map. Now would you please go? I'm freezing my butt off here."

Seth's tone became hard. "How do I know the ring you showed me in California wasn't a fake?"

"Trust me. I can tell. My mother has more diamond rings than Elizabeth Taylor. It was your ring, all right."

Seth looked unconvinced.

"Play Columbo. Check the one she's wearing, Seth. See for yourself."

"I'm not sure I could tell. I mean, I'm no jeweler."

Diana felt herself losing patience. She adjusted her towel, took a deep breath, and prayed she wouldn't say something she'd regret. "Seth," she said softly, reasonably, "have you forgotten about Austin? Set aside the whole question of the ring. Assume I'm lying about it, although Lord knows why I would. What about *Austin?*"

Seth gazed at the yellowed linoleum. "You know, I could replace this for you guys," he said vaguely.

"*Seth.* Track with me here. What about Austin?"

He nodded slowly. "I know. I know I have to confront her about him. I just . . . wanted to hold her for a minute, be with her like nothing had changed."

"Nothing?" Diana exploded. "Everything's changed, Seth! Have you forgotten how furious you were this weekend? What happened to all your righteous indignation?" She lowered her voice. "Have you forgotten what went on between us? What was I? Just a cheap stand-in?" She went to him and grabbed his arms. "She loves Austin, Seth. Don't be fooled. I've seen them together, laughing and whispering. I've seen him with his hands all over her."

She could feel him tense. "I don't know what to believe anymore," he said.

"Believe your ears, Seth. Confront her. You'll hear her lies and then you'll know."

Seth gave a slight, almost imperceptible nod. "There's some kind of beach party tonight, Marquez said. I'll get Summer alone and I'll confront her. I will."

"I hope so, Seth," Diana said. "I can't go on this way. And neither can you. Now beat it. I still have to volumize."

His gaze locked on her, seeming for the first time to see her. "You smell like tangerines," he said.

"You like it?"

"Yeah, I do. Summer's hair always smells like tangerines too."

12

Diver Moves In and Austin Moves On

Austin lay sprawled on his dilapidated couch, watching as Diver unpacked his meager possessions.

"Man, you do live light, don't you?" he said. He took another swig of his beer, one of several he planned on consuming before the evening was over.

Diver shrugged. "A sleeping bag, a cup, a fork, a toothbrush, a bar of soap. What else does a man need?"

"A loaf of bread, a jug of wine, and someone other than thou," Austin replied. "Speaking of, want a beer?"

"I don't drink. It disturbs my *wa.*"

"Your *wa,* you say?"

Diver shrugged. "My inner harmony. I used to think girls disturbed my *wa* too. But then I met Marquez."

"By the way, she called right before you got here. Something about a party over on Turtle Beach at sunset."

"Hmm. Want to come?"

"Nope. Gotta work." Austin consulted his watch. "As a matter of fact, I'm already late. And anyway, your sister might be at the party. As it happens, she's been disturbing my *wa* all to hell."

"I know. I'm sorry about that."

Austin watched Diver meticulously reroll his sleeping bag. It left a sprinkling of white sand on the floor.

"You're a man of few words, Diver," Austin said. "A fine quality in a roommate. Although I wouldn't have complained if you'd brought a state-of-the-art stereo along with your fork and your toothbrush."

"I didn't have electricity at my last place. It was in a tree."

"Somehow that doesn't particularly surprise me."

Diver scanned a pile of CDs on a bookcase. "I notice a lot of classical cello CDs."

"You into classical?"

"I'll listen to pretty much anything." Diver grinned. "Especially the ocean." He pulled a CD off the shelf. "You've got a lot of these. Caleb Reed. Is he good?"

"Was. He's my dad."

"He's . . . gone?"

"In a manner of speaking. He has Huntington's disease. He's what you might call going."

Diver nodded solemnly. He returned the CD to the shelf gently, almost reverently.

The simple gesture touched Austin. When the subject of his dad came up, most people mouthed platitudes or asked prying questions. But Diver knew better than to do either. Yeah, he was going to be an okay roommate.

Too bad he would also serve as a constant reminder of Summer.

Austin crumpled his beer can and stood a little unsteadily. "Well, I'm off to ply my trade. You got a key, right?"

Diver nodded. "You sure you don't want to come by the party tonight?"

"Real sure." Austin grabbed a pen and notepad for work. "Make yourself at home. I'll see you later."

Outside, the air carried the fresh tang of the ocean. Austin made his way down the winding streets of Coconut Key at a leisurely pace. He wasn't in any hurry. He didn't really care if they fired him at Jitters. One way or another, he was going to have to find a different job anyway. He couldn't keep working there, not with Summer so close by.

Maybe he should move to Boca Beach, up the coast. His dad was in the hospital there, and Austin could visit him more often. It would probably do more good for Austin than for his dad, who was pretty far gone.

Still, it seemed like the right thing to do. Stick around for the death vigil.

And while he was at it, get a glimpse of the future.

Suddenly the street began to sway. The beer and the sun were making him a little dizzy, he told himself—that was all. He leaned against a palm tree, the spiny trunk like knives against his back.

The reality of his situation hit him like that every so often, sneak attacks that left him winded and disoriented. He *knew* the truth, of course. Every waking moment he knew it. But he only *felt* it now and then, often when he least expected it.

He resumed walking, more slowly now. A beautiful blond girl in a string bikini skated past, but he barely noticed her.

He wondered, not for the first time, if he should have told Summer the truth. It wasn't as if she couldn't have handled it. She would have been great. A real trouper.

And it would have been nice, so nice, to have someone to share the burden with. His brother knew, and his mom, but it was different with them. They saw the world through the dark lens of their own experience. When his brother learned he'd inherited the same defective gene that had caused Austin's father's slow demise, he'd seriously considered killing himself.

No, they could see the world only in terms of their own genetic bad luck.

But Summer would have been different. She would have come up with hopeful things to say. "It will be years and years before you have any symptoms yourself, Austin. They're doing all kinds of exciting genetic research. You can't give up hope, not this soon."

It would have been great to hear someone say those things. Even if they weren't necessarily true.

But he'd lied to her. Said he'd gone to the genetics clinic and passed the test with flying colors. He'd wanted to spare her the knowledge. It would have been cruel to tell her.

Of course, if he'd really been noble, he would have walked out of her life for good a long time ago and never come back. It was probably wrong for him to have tried to get her back, knowing what he knew.

He paused in front of the Victorian house where Jitters was located. The café looked busy, full of loud tourists. He stared up at the third-floor balcony, Summer's balcony. There was no sign of her.

She was gone, lost to him.

He wondered if he could have fought harder to keep her. Probably, he decided. But in his heart he knew it was fairer to her to let her go.

Maybe this was just how things were meant to turn out. He didn't bother asking why. He didn't try to find an explanation—fate, the stars, bad karma, bad luck. That was one thing his father's slow dying had taught him: Asking why was a waste of breath.

13

The Case of the Incredible
Shrinking Knuckle

Diver skirted the foaming surf, enjoying the feel of the wet, packed sand as it first resisted and then gave way to his feet. The quiet water was surprisingly warm. The first stars of the evening glittered low on the horizon, delicate pinpricks of golden light.

He loved the beach. It was home. Sometimes he wondered if he really had been born in Minnesota. Here at the edge of the world, where the land gave out and slipped into the sea, was the only place he truly felt at peace.

Two girls jogged by on the sand. As soon as they were past him, one of the girls let loose an earsplitting wolf whistle. Diver looked back, and they picked up their speed, giggling musically.

He shook his head. Will, one of the guys at his old job, had claimed Diver was a "babe magnet." And sometimes Diver wondered if there was some strange truth to it. Girls did seem to be awfully interested in him. It should have been flattering, he supposed. But it always made him a little uncomfortable when some girl, an utter stranger, made a move on him. How he looked on the outside, after all, had nothing to do with who he was on the inside. It always surprised him that girls didn't understand that better.

He stooped to pick up a nice unbroken shell. He heard the soft shuffle of footsteps in the sand and looked up to see a figure, a girl, approaching him with a determined gait.

He kept low, hoping to avoid another embarrassing flirtation. In the scant starlight, it took him a minute to register the short, stylish blond hair and pretty features.

Caroline.

Diver tossed the shell aside and stood. There was no need to panic. He'd brushed her off easily at the hospital. If she pressed any more, he'd just shrug and deny whatever she had to say.

"Paul. I was hoping you'd show up tonight."

She stood before him, hands on hips, much smaller than he was but intimidating nevertheless. She was wearing a black one-piece suit and a black nylon windbreaker. She very nearly blended into the night.

Diver gave a laugh. "Boy, I wish I could help you out. I mean, any guy in his right mind would have loved to have you for a next-door neighbor. But like I said, you've got the wrong guy. I've never even been to Virginia."

She smiled coolly. "That's too bad," she said in her smooth southern accent. "And here I went to all the trouble of having this faxed to me. On my vacation, no less. What a shame." Caroline reached into the pocket of her windbreaker and retrieved a neatly folded piece of paper. "Still, you might want to read it anyway. Just to be sure."

Diver took the paper from her. Even in the darkness, he could see it was a copy of a newspaper article.

"I know it's kind of dark to read, but you can probably make out the pictures just fine."

Diver didn't have to look. He'd saved the same clipping. It was yellow around the edges now and crisp to the touch.

The fire. What remained of his house.

And beside that photo, another, smaller one. From his seventh-grade yearbook, a blond, blue-eyed boy with an attitude, refusing to smile for the school photographer.

The caption read "Missing Youth, Suspect in Arson Death."

Caroline touched his arm. Her fingers were cool. Her smile was pretty, believable the same way an artificial Christmas tree seems real from far away.

"I'd really like to talk to you, Paul."

It wasn't a request.

"I have nothing to say to you." Diver pushed past her.

She ran to catch up and grabbed his arm. He stopped.

"You know, I'm thinking that a murder suspect doesn't really have a lot of negotiating room," Caroline said, Sunday-school teacher sweet. "Tomorrow afternoon, your place."

Diver closed his eyes. "All right. Just . . . don't say anything to anyone till then. Deal?"

"Oh, your secret's safe with me, Paul." She let go of his arm. "It'll be fun. Just a couple of neighbors chatting about old times."

"I'm staying—"

"I know where you're staying." Caroline started back toward the party. "I've done my homework. Now come on. We've got a beach party to attend. And I even promise to call you Diver."

☆   ☆   ☆

Summer took Seth's hand and pulled him toward the water. "Come on, you big baby," she teased. "The water's incredibly warm. I know you're used to mellow Pacific Ocean water now, but this'll have to do."

She pulled Seth in while the others, sitting on the sand, laughed and applauded.

When the water was waist deep, Seth wrapped his arms around Summer and held her close as the gentle waves nudged them.

"This is nice," he said.

"Are you sure?" Summer asked. "You've been so quiet. Maybe it wasn't such a good idea, coming here to the party with all these people."

She glanced back at the beach. Blythe, Caroline, and some other people, friends of Blythe and people from the apartment building, were gathered around a small bonfire. Janet Jackson was playing on the portable CD player someone had brought along. Marquez and Diver were off by themselves, slow-dancing. Two other couples were dancing at the edge of the water, including Diana and some guy who was a high-school friend of Blythe's. The guy was cute in a gawky way, but he wasn't Diana's type. She was probably just being polite.

It had been a nice party, with good food and lots of laughs. And in a way it had been a relief to have a lot of people around to keep things from getting too difficult with Seth. It didn't hurt to have the whole defensive lineup there, but Summer knew it couldn't last much longer.

They needed to talk. All evening Seth had been watching her doubtfully and speaking too politely, as if she were his just-arrived mail-order bride.

Maybe it didn't mean anything. Diana and Diver had been quiet, too. Maybe it was just the rich food and the hot night air and the endless whisper of the waves lulling people into silence.

"I guess I haven't been very talkative," Seth admitted. "I've had a lot on my mind." He took a deep breath. "So. Tell me the truth. Have you missed me?"

She tried to ignore the edge in his voice. "Of course I have. Have you missed me?"

"More than you know. What have you been up to?"

Again the harsh tone. "You know, just . . . job-hunting, mostly. Unsuccessfully. I have another interview tomorrow, though." She crossed her fingers. "Maybe this time they'll take pity on me."

Seth stared at her hand, the crossed fingers, the little fake ring.

"Summer," he said softly. "I love you."

He pulled her close and kissed her for a long time. It wasn't like his familiar kisses. It was shy, the tentative, hopeful kiss of a first date.

He let her go and took her left hand. He cupped it in both of his and lifted it to his lips. His hands, to her surprise, were trembling.

He kissed her fingers, then pulled back, admiring her ring.

"It looks nice in the moonlight, doesn't it?" he said.

She nodded but said nothing.

"I was worried when I got it," Seth continued. "You know, would it fit, would it be the right one. But then I saw it and I knew. The jeweler told me it was one of a kind—did I tell you that?"

He reached for the ring, clasped the band with his fingers, and tugged a little. "It's loose. That's weird. I could barely get it past your knuckle, remember?"

Summer swallowed. "Guess I've lost weight."

"In your knuckle?" Seth laughed, but it wasn't exactly a happy laugh. He pulled a little harder on the ring.

Summer yanked her hand away. "Seth, you can't take it off."

"Why not?" he demanded. "Haven't you ever?"

"No. It would be bad luck. I'm sure there's some kind of old wives' tale about that. Like seeing the bride in her gown before the wedding."

Seth was staring at her. His dark eyes glowed in the moonlight. She shivered even though the air was hot. She had a queasy feeling in her gut, the one she got when she knew she was making a mess of things.

"Let me see the ring, Summer."

"Why?"

Seth held out his hand. Summer hesitated. After a moment she slipped the ring off her finger.

He held it up to the moonlight, the shining emblem of her stupidity and weakness.

Why hadn't she just told him the truth, told him everything? There was a lesson there somewhere. Don't avoid pain—just get it over with like an adult.

Or at least don't go buying replacement rings at Woolworth.

Like a savvy buyer, Seth studied the ring, squinting at it in the darkness. He was looking for something. He *knew*.

How did he know? Could he have read it in her eyes? She wasn't exactly a poker face. Had he noticed the cheap setting? The loose fit?

Could Diana have let the truth slip?

He ran the tip of his index finger inside the band. "There's engraving," he pronounced. He seemed satisfied, but she saw disappointment in his eyes. "I didn't have your ring engraved," he pointed out flatly. "Did you have the ring engraved?"

"No."

"Then what does this say?"

Summer sighed. It was over. She'd been caught. She deserved her fate.

"I believe," she said quietly, "it says 'Made in Taiwan.'"

Seth drew back his arm. With a great heave, he hurled the ring far out into the black water.

It landed without a sound. Strange, Summer thought, for such a big moment. There should have been a huge splash, maybe even a tidal wave.

"Tell me it all," Seth said.

14

They Say Confession Is Good for the Soul

They headed back to the beach and walked in silence for a while, until the noise of the party had evaporated in the night air.

"I was painting the door," Summer began.

She sat on the beach. Seth sat too, leaving a wide space between them. They both stared out at the black, sluggish ocean, avoiding each other's gaze.

"Painting," Seth repeated doubtfully.

"I'd already gotten some paint on the ring once," Summer said, "and I didn't want to get any more on it. I was afraid it might not come off."

"Not come off," Seth repeated again.

"Well, how should I know? I've never had a diamond before. I'm not adult enough to have real jewelry, Seth. Before we got engaged, the most expensive thing I'd ever owned was that pin in the shape of Minnesota my aunt Ethel gave me. And I never wore that, except to family reunions. And Aunt Ethel's funeral. I mean, how the heck was I supposed to know?"

She took note of the hysterical pitch in her voice and resolved to stay calm. She was a criminal spilling it all to a cop. A penitent confessing to a priest. There was no point in getting all emotional about it.

"So you took off the ring—"

"And I put it on the windowsill in a Dixie cup, and the next thing I knew the cup was empty and the ring was gone. We searched the apartment for hours, and outside too. Under the window, in the bushes, you name it."

"The gutters?"

"Diver checked those."

"Under the bed, that sort of thing? It could have rolled anywhere, right?"

"Trust me, I looked. I was frantic, Seth. But I kept thinking that there had to be a logical explanation, that it'd turn up, that it *had* to turn up. People don't just suddenly lose their engagement rings, except maybe in movies." She sighed. "Of course, usually those are comedies."

"Go on."

"Well, the thing is, I didn't want to tell you because I thought you'd take it as some kind of omen. Like it meant something. Sort of a Freudian slip."

She stole a glance at Seth. He was nodding slowly, reserving judgment.

"So when you called and said you were coming," Summer continued, "Marquez and I went out and tried to find a duplicate ring. We must have gone to every store on the Key. And then finally, when I was just about to give up, I found the perfect imitation."

"The one I just threw into the ocean."

"We found it in the jewelry section at Woolworth."

Seth winced.

"I mean, it's not like it was anywhere near as beautiful," Summer hastened to add. "But I thought it might be enough to get by until . . . until I found the real one. Which probably sounds incredibly stupid and naive, not to mention really, really chicken."

"Yeah. Especially the chicken part."

"I didn't want to upset you, Seth. I know how hard you worked for that ring. And I felt like such a jerk. The truth is," she sighed, "some squirrel probably ate it. Or some rat sneaked it away to its nest."

"That does seem possible," Seth said. "Some large, conniving rat."

"What?"

"Nothing."

"I'm sorry, Seth. I'm so sorry." She took a deep, shuddery breath. "But there's more."

The hard part. The really, really hard part.

Seth turned to her, waiting, his jaw clenched. He almost seemed to be anticipating her words. But of course he didn't know how awful they would be.

Summer looked away. "There's something you should know, Seth. It's like the ring . . . I should have just come out with it. But when someone you love is far away, it's harder. It's hard to say certain things over the phone." She groaned. "I have no excuse. I just didn't want you to get the wrong, you know, impression—"

"Say it already, Summer."

"Austin Reed moved here."

She waited for the furious, shocked accusations of betrayal, but none came. Seth just gazed out at the ocean, rocking slightly in the sand.

"He was here on Coconut Key even before Diana and Marquez and I found our apartment. He works at Jitters—you know, the café downstairs?"

"And?"

"And that's all."

"You've been seeing him?" His voice was choked.

"No, I mean yes, I mean I've seen him, yeah. He's sort of hard to avoid. But I made it very clear to him that whatever we had is completely over."

"Do you still have feelings for him? The way you did last spring?"

Summer considered. She'd told so many half-truths, done so much evading, that it was starting to come naturally to her. But she wanted to clear the air once and for all. Even if it meant causing more pain.

"I did have feelings for him, Seth. I don't think you can care about someone and then, bam, suddenly stop caring. But I realized something important when I was sorting through all this." She slipped her hand through his. "We are engaged, Seth."

"And this was news to you?"

She stared up at the vast expanse of stars. "Do you ever think about what that means? It means you and me, together until we die. It means loyalty to each other above all else." She smiled wistfully. "And it means forgiveness—at least I hope it means that."

For a while they didn't speak. The waves rolled back and forth over the sand, waiting, it seemed, as impatiently as Summer was waiting.

Finally Seth stood. He looked down at her. She could not read his expression.

"You should have told me all this."

"I know."

"How can we trust each other if we're not completely honest?"

"I know. I didn't want to hurt you. Again."

"It's going to take me some time, Summer. I have to sort through all this."

She nodded.

"Maybe—" Behind her she heard movement. She turned to see someone, a tall guy, walking down the beach at the water's edge. Stumbling was more like it.

"He looks drunk," Summer said.

"Plastered."

The figure grew larger, clearer. He was humming to himself.

Suddenly he stopped.

"Shummer," he said.

"Oh, God," Summer whispered.

Austin sauntered over, nearly tripping on his own feet.

"Seth, let me talk to him alone, okay? He's drunk. There's no telling how he might act."

"Maybe this is a good thing," Seth said darkly. "We can clear the air at last."

Austin paused before them, staring at Summer blearily. "Shummer," he whispered.

"Hi, Austin," she whispered.

He stared unsteadily at Seth.

"You remember me, Austin," Seth said. "We met during spring break. It's me. Sheth."

15

The Whole Truth and Anything But

I have to say, your timing's perfect," Seth said. "We were just discussing you."

"I'm flattered."

"Don't be."

"Austin," Summer said gently, "this isn't really a good time—"

Austin frowned, then swayed. "I came for the party. Diver said there was a party."

"The party's down the beach," Summer said, but Austin just stood there, eyeing Seth as though Austin were a scientist who'd just discovered a new and intriguing species.

Seth turned to Summer. "Isn't this the part where we duel for the fair maiden? Is that what you want, Summer?"

"I'm really sort of a pacifist," Austin said. He swayed a little more, then plopped onto the sand with a grunt. "Could play poker for her, if ya want."

"No, that's too lowbrow," Seth said sarcastically. "Summer needs a nineties way to choose her man. How about earnings potential? What do you want to do, Austin?"

Austin lay back on the sand, considering. "You mean when I grow up?"

"A big if, I grant you. What's your game plan?"

"I'm going to be a starving poet. Suffer for my art. Then die a tragic early death. Or else I'll write for Hollywood."

"Well, I plan to become an architect and have my own firm someday. I'd like to see six figures by the time I'm thirty."

Summer crossed her arms over her chest. "Since when?"

"Since always."

"Seth, you're being ridiculous."

"Okay, then. We'll look at the whole picture. You want to have kids, Austin?"

Austin narrowed his eyes. "With you?"

Seth grimaced.

"Well," Austin said, "kids, I don't know. They're kind of like a long-term commitment.

122

But I wouldn't mind a dog. Maybe one of those big, sloppy pound dogs. . . ."

Seth rolled his eyes. "I'm getting at least two kids. A boy and a girl."

"So," Austin said, rolling onto his side, "you can just, like . . . order them from a catalog?"

Seth sighed loudly. "How about your education?" he pressed.

"I watch *Jeopardy!* every afternoon."

"I'm going for my advanced degree at UW."

"University of Weeniedom?" Austin let loose an impressively loud burp. "A nice enough little preschool, I guess." He glanced at Summer slyly. "Although I hear Carlson's even better."

"Say what?"

"Austin," Summer warned.

Austin sat up and waved Seth off extravagantly. "Never mind. Look, I came for the party, not for Shummer. You already won."

Seth glanced at Summer. "What do you mean?"

"She chose you and blew me off. Loyalty, honor, all that good stuff." He shrugged. His body was loose, jointless. "It's just as well. I'm what they call in insurance circles a bad risk."

Seth stared from Austin to Summer and back again. "You're telling me the truth, man?"

Austin offered up a goofy smile. "Yeah, I know, I had a hard time believing it too."

"I told you, Seth," Summer whispered.

For the first time Seth seemed to have come to a conclusion. He nodded firmly. "I believe you. I do." He reached out his hand to Summer. "Come on. Let's go back to your place."

Summer jerked her head toward Austin, who was lying on his back, arms spread, making sand angels.

"We can't leave him."

"Leave him," Austin advised. "He'sh fine."

"I can't, Austin. Remember that other time? The time you went swimming at night over spring break?"

It seemed like ages ago, but it had been only a few months. Austin had been upset over his father and gone swimming, half intending to drown himself. Summer had saved him, but not without nearly drowning herself in the process.

Seth let out a long exhalation, slowly shaking his head. He held out his hand to Austin. "Come on, buddy. We're taking you home."

"A threeshome?" Austin inquired.

Seth gave a rueful laugh. "Yeah, Austin. Something like that."

★　　★　　★

At two in the morning Diana eased open the door to the apartment. The lights were out, which meant Summer and Marquez were already asleep. Good thing. She was exhausted and angry and not in the mood for another episode of *The Seth and Summer Show*.

She locked the door behind her and tossed her keys on the counter. Moonlight streamed through the balcony doors.

She'd spent the whole evening watching Summer and Seth together. Hoping that Seth would take note, she'd even pretended to flirt with some guy named P. J., an old friend of Blythe's. When she'd danced with the guy, he'd smelled of licorice and sweat and held her too close. Diana had watched over her shoulder while Summer and Seth went swimming in the ocean. Swimming and kissing.

She wondered where Seth was staying that night. She wondered if she really wanted to know the answer to that question. She was starting to realize that ignorance was sometimes bliss.

"Where've you been?" a low voice inquired.

Diana jumped, her hand to her heart. Seth was sitting on the couch in the dark.

"You scared me, Seth," Diana hissed. "What are you doing lurking around there? Why aren't you with Summer?" She said the name with just the right touch of sarcasm.

"How about a little poolside chat, Diana?"

"I'm tired."

"We could do it here," Seth said in a hushed voice, "but I'm not sure you want Summer to hear what I have to say to you about you and her ring."

Diana sighed. She might as well get it over with. "Fine. Whatever. Let's go to the pool and you can tell me how you believe all Summer's nice little lies."

Seth didn't speak all the way down to the backyard. The pool was unlit, save for the silver moonlight frosting the water. A dragonfly struggled across the surface, unable to free itself from the water's hold. Diana knelt down and scooped it out. It buzzed away in wild loops.

"You lied to me, Diana." Seth said it wearily, like a disappointed teacher. His hands were on his hips.

When he wanted to, he could be downright parental, Diana reflected.

"Summer lost that ring. She didn't take it off because she wanted to break up with me."

"So that's the story," Diana said. She sat on the edge of the pool, dangling her legs in the warm water. "And you're buying it. Seth, you are nothing if not eternally gullible. You are the ultimate used-car salesman's fantasy. You'll buy anything as long as it comes wrapped up in a pretty package."

"One thing about Summer, Diana. Unlike you, she's a lousy liar. She told me how the ring disappeared while she was painting. The story was too Summer-like not to be true." He sat down on the edge of a pool chair, hands clasped between his knees. "The thing is, she didn't know the ending to the story. The part where you somehow found the ring and flew it all the way to California."

Diana's mind was in overdrive, searching for ways out of the corner she'd boxed herself into. But nothing could help her. She'd trapped herself. "Fine, whatever," she snapped, her tense voice betraying her outward calm. "Believe what you want to believe, Seth." She hesitated. "So . . . did you tell her about me and the ring?"

"No. I didn't see the point in hurting her."

"Very noble. Of course, there's still the little matter of Austin Reed."

"Funny you should bring him up. Guess who crashed the party this evening—Austin himself."

"Any bloodshed?"

"Sorry to disappoint you. He was right-eously drunk. He told me just what Summer told me," Seth said, sounding way too much like a prosecutor going in for the kill. "She chose *me*. She wanted *me*, Diana."

"Interesting. Did he also tell you how he pawed her by this very pool a few days ago?"

Seth gave her a long-suffering look.

"You saw the picture, Seth. Austin and Summer, right here. Extremely close together. Some might say intimately close. And that's just the time I was able to capture it on film. Who knows what went on with them behind closed doors?"

"This is why you're so good, Diana." Seth wagged a finger at her. "There's just enough truth mixed in with your fiction to make it compelling. Summer's not wearing her ring, true enough. Austin's here in Coconut Key, true enough. And yes, I bought your version of events hook, line, and sinker. But it wasn't the whole truth. I'm starting to realize you're not very good at the whole truth, Diana."

"I told you the truth about my feelings for you." Her voice was soft and indistinct. "That was the whole truth."

"Maybe," Seth said. "I suppose I'll never really know."

She could hear, in his indifferent tone, his condescension. Seth was slipping from her grasp. Panic hammered at her. And when Diana felt panicked, she fought back tooth and nail, like any cornered animal.

She stood, eyeing him with cold disdain, waiting until she saw a hint of worry.

"You know, Seth," she said, "it seems to me that I'm not the only person here who has trouble with the concept of the whole truth. You've been known to leave out part of the story yourself."

"What's that supposed to mean?"

"It means you're a hypocrite. It means you used me. It means"—she turned to go—"this isn't over yet. You want the whole truth? Fine. You know what they say. Watch out what you wish for, Seth. You might just get it."

16

Just One Big Happy Family

*M*arquez checked the mileage counter on her exercise bike. "Wimp," she muttered. A couple of days off and she'd completely lost her stride. Not only that, her morning weigh-in had been positively devastating.

She'd been eating, that's why. And to get Diver and Summer off her case, she'd completely blown her exercise strategy. If she let them have their way, she'd blimp up like a balloon at the Macy's Thanksgiving Day parade.

She pedaled even faster. Sweat trickled down her chest. Diana was still asleep, Summer was in the shower, and Seth was crashed out on the couch, oblivious. For once she could work off some calories without the diet narcs on her case.

At the beach party the night before, Diver had been all over her about going to counseling. When he talked to her at all, that was. For most of the evening he'd been busy gawking at that Caroline girl. Beautiful, skinny Caroline. All night they'd eyed each other.

Marquez was not an idiot. She could see what was going on. And if there'd been any doubt, the way Diver had clammed up was all the evidence she needed. He'd been quiet, even by his standards.

She was losing him, she was sure of it. Someday soon she was going to walk in on him and Caroline, just the way she'd walked in on J.T. and that slut.

Sure, Diver swore everything was fine, swore he loved her. But he was like Summer that way. Too nice to say the truth of things.

She'd just clocked another mile when Diana emerged from her bedroom. She had on her red silk robe. Her hair was mussed, and there were dark, shiny circles under her eyes. That was pretty rough around the edges for Diana. She usually arose looking as though she'd just had a *Seventeen* makeover.

"Is this fresh coffee?" Diana muttered, holding up the pot.

"I have nothing to say to you, Diana," Marquez replied.

"And that would be, like, a punishment?"

Summer came out of the bathroom dressed in a slinky blue sundress. She took one look at Marquez on the bike and groaned. "You're not overdoing it, are you?"

"Not if the scale is any indication."

"Marquez—"

"All right, all right." Marquez slowed her pedaling. "I just need to cool down. What are you all dressed up for, anyway?"

"My companion interview."

"Seems to me you have plenty of companions," Diana said under her breath.

"What?" Summer asked.

"Nothing."

Summer leaned over the back of the couch and kissed Seth lightly on the lips. He opened his eyes. "Excellent wake-up call," he said, yawning. "Hey, you look great."

"Does anyone know if this is new coffee?" Diana demanded.

"I made it a while ago," Summer said. "It's probably kind of bitter."

"Perfect," Diana said. She popped a cup in

the microwave, cast a dark glance at Seth, and headed for the bathroom.

"What's the matter with her?" Summer asked.

Marquez shrugged. "Let's just say some of her best-laid plans fell through."

"Well, I'm off," Summer said, grabbing her purse. "Wish me luck. Do I look like companion material?"

"You do to me," Seth said with a leer. "Hey, you sure this guy just wants you to, like, run errands and stuff?"

"No, Seth. He wants me to clean the house wearing a French maid costume." Summer rolled her eyes. "He was in a really bad accident. He's in a wheelchair."

"But his hands work, right?"

"Seth, please shut up. I am desperate. It's this or I get a job at Jitters."

"Whoa. Knock 'em dead."

Summer snapped her fingers. "Marquez. Before I forget, the nurse at the hospital said you should call to confirm that you're going to the counseling session tomorrow, remember?"

Marquez just kept pedaling. She suddenly realized that she'd already come to a decision.

"You're not backing out?" Summer asked.

"Look, maybe I'll go next week. I'm just not in the mood, okay?"

"But you promised."

"Well, I lied. God knows I'm not the only person around this place who's done it." Marquez was pleased when both Summer and Seth looked equally uncomfortable.

Still, Summer wouldn't go down without a fight. "Marquez, please go, for me. For Diver."

"Summer, I am a big girl and I don't want to be nagged. Nagging would *not* be a good idea." She gave Summer her best back-off look. "*Not*, I repeat, a good idea. Got it?"

Summer sighed. "We'll talk about this later."

"It's going to be a very brief, very one-sided conversation."

"We'll talk," was all Summer would say. She kissed Seth one more time. "I'm glad we're okay," she said.

"Me too. Real glad."

Before leaving, Summer cast one last disapproving, hopeful, plaintive, annoyed look at Marquez. It was amazing. The girl could convey more guilt trips with her blue eyes than all the nuns at Marquez's junior high combined.

When the door closed behind Summer, Seth sat up, rubbing his eyes. "What did you mean," he asked, jerking his head toward the bathroom door, "about Diana's plans falling through?"

Marquez climbed off the bike, testing her rubbery legs. "'Should auld acquaintance be forgot—'"

Seth gulped. "New Year's?"

"New Year's."

"You didn't tell Summer?"

"I haven't yet. But let me just say this. You and Diana had better behave yourselves, or I may be feeling a lot more talkative."

"There's nothing between Diana and me, Marquez."

"I guess she just flew out to California for the scenery?"

Seth actually flushed.

"Yeah, that's what I figured." Marquez wiped her brow with a towel. "Look, this apartment has more secrets in it than my eighth-grade diary. I can't even keep track anymore. Let's just keep things simple. You behave, I'll keep my mouth shut. Deal?"

"I love Summer, you know that."

"And Diana loves you. And Austin loves Summer, I'm guessing. You're like rabbits, all of you. In heat. In the spring. Just get a grip on the hormones, and I'll mind my own business."

Seth laughed. "You have my solemn oath that my hormones are under complete control."

"You're a guy, right?"

"Last time I checked."

"Then your hormones will be under control around the time you're six feet under."

Seth got up to pour himself a cup of coffee. He turned to Marquez, hesitating. "You know, that counseling stuff . . . Summer really thinks it might be a good thing to give it a shot."

"That," Marquez said, shaking a finger at Seth, "would be an example of business that doesn't need any minding from you."

"Sorry."

"Apology accepted. Now do me a favor."

"What?"

"Go in there and ask Countess Dracula to hurry up with her shower. I'm not speaking to her."

Seth grinned. "You're afraid of her?"

"Not as long as I'm wearing a clove of garlic around my neck. You?"

"No." Seth gazed at the door almost wistfully. "Diana's just complicated, that's all."

"Calculus is complicated, Seth. Diana's easy to understand. She's evil. Pure and simple."

"Well, I'm glad somebody understands her," Seth said wearily. "I know I never will."

Marquez nodded. "Were you . . . you know . . . ever really in love with her?"

"You think calculus is complicated?" Seth laughed sadly. "I'm still working on that one."

17

References Available on Request

Summer checked the address she'd written on the paper. It was in an exclusive residential area, a private enclave on a sort of mini-island off the key.

When she'd called about the companion ad, a nurse had answered. The patient (as she'd referred to him) was eighteen. He'd been in a near-fatal car accident while visiting Germany. His family lived in New England, but they were renting this house in the Keys for his rehabilitation. He wanted to recover in private, away from prying eyes. He'd suffered injuries to his spine, his right leg, his face, even his vocal cords. He was partially paralyzed. He was a nice boy, quiet, not demanding like some of the nurse's former clients. He needed someone to read to him, run errands, keep him company.

Did Summer have a résumé? Any nursing experience? Any experience, period?

Summer turned the corner onto the small road that skirted the beach. The sun was searing, the sky cloudless. She wondered if this was a waste of time. She took out the résumé in her purse, the one she'd put together the previous night. It was handwritten, since she didn't have access to a typewriter, and on lined paper, since she'd forgotten to buy any typing paper.

Summer Ann Smith
142 Lido Lane, Apartment 301
Coconut Key, Florida 33031

Telephone: I don't have one yet, but the phone company says this week for sure or next week for absolute sure. My cousin's phone is 555-8761 if you need to get in touch with me, but she'll probably answer. Her name's Diana.

Job Objective: Companion.

Education: Graduate of Bloomington High School, Bloomington, Minnesota.

Activities: High school honor society, three years; choir; yearbook; copy editor of *The Bloomington Bugle* (school newspaper).

Job History:

— Five years baby-sitting experience, including regular care for triplets. Played, changed diapers, made meals, supervised homework. Developed excellent supervisory skills and ability to make killer macaroni and cheese.

— One summer waiting tables, Crab 'n' Conch, Crab Claw Key, Florida. Served patrons, worked as hostess, did side work, took inventory, did extensive cleaning. Developed public relations skills and superior upper arm strength.

Available for work: Immediately.

References: Available on request.

Summer sighed. It looked, she had to admit, pretty unimpressive. Even she wouldn't have hired herself. And she was her own best reference.

It was her own fault for waiting till the last minute. She'd written the résumé the night before, after the beach party. She'd been worried and distracted after her big discussion with Seth and after escorting Austin back to his apartment.

Summer paused to slip off her sandals. She crossed the street and headed to the beach. She made it a policy to avoid wearing shoes whenever possible, and besides, the hot sand felt heavenly.

She passed the spot where she and Seth had talked during the party. She should have felt relieved after getting things out in the open with him. She'd thought making a clear choice would have simplified things, but after seeing Austin depressed and drunk, she'd felt awful. Maybe making a choice wasn't the hard part. Maybe living with the aftermath was.

Did she feel this way because she'd made such a mess of things? Or because she'd come to the wrong conclusion about Seth and Austin?

She watched a group of children racing to finish a sand castle. No, Seth was her fiancé. She loved him. She owed her loyalty to him.

She wondered if it was a good sign that she had to keep repeating the same mantra over and over again, reminding herself of the reasons she and Seth belonged together.

She crossed back to the street, put her sandals on, and turned down a private dirt road. A narrow wooden bridge spanned the water that separated the key from Eden Shores, where her job interview would take place.

Seth was leaving the next day. He'd told her he'd done what he needed to do, coming back to touch base with her. He was going back to finish up his internship. Then the rest of the summer would be theirs together.

She was definitely going to discuss the college situation with him before he left. Technically she could wait; after all, she didn't yet know if Carlson was going to accept her. But she'd learned her lesson about avoiding hard confrontations. Better to do it right away, even if her application was rejected later. He would be upset and would see it as a betrayal. But Seth would just have to understand that when it came to her education, she had to listen to her own heart.

At least she felt comfortable with this choice. She knew it was the right thing. Austin had helped her realize she'd decided against going to Carlson because she was afraid of failing there.

She would tell Seth that he could reapply to Carlson the next semester. Maybe if his grades at UW were good, Carlson would take him and they could still spend most of their college years together. But she was not going to go to UW just to make him happy or just because he hadn't been accepted to Carlson. Not even after all that had happened between them. She couldn't live her life trying to please Seth.

A uniformed guard in a gatehouse had to make a call before she was allowed to cross the bridge. It was her first taste of Eden Shores, a place people in Coconut Key talked about in hushed tones. Lushly lined with palms, it was home to maybe two dozen estates, huge pastel fortresses with giant windows, giant pools, giant privacy walls, and giant Dobermans standing guard. A small but exclusive yacht club claimed the south end of the islet.

It made her a little uncomfortable. She'd never really known any rich people, unless you counted Adam Merrick, the senator's son she'd dated briefly the previous summer. He'd seemed like a perfectly normal guy—that is, if you could have two hundred bathrooms in your house and still be perfectly normal. Of course, in the end he'd turned out to be a complete dirtbag. It seemed that having money didn't necessarily mean you also had character.

The perfectly manicured main avenue was empty save for a few gardeners sweating profusely in the wet heat. Summer checked the address again. The house was at the end of a cul-de-sac, an imposing building made of peach stucco. She shook the sand out of her sandals, smoothed down her hair, and rang the bell.

The door swung open to reveal a portly butler. His few remaining strands of silver hair were combed over his shiny bald head. His bulging gray eyes reminded Summer of a cartoon fish. He nodded gravely. "May I help you?"

"I'm here about the companion job. My name is Summer Smith. I'm sorry I'm a little early, but I walked and I wasn't sure how long it would take, because I've never been here before."

The butler indulged a smile, the corners of his lips twitching just a bit. "Come in, Ms. Smith," he said, revealing a clipped New England accent. "You'll be speaking with Ms. Rodriguez on the lanai."

Summer followed him to an airy screened porch overlooking the ocean. It was furnished with white wicker rockers surrounding a rectangular lap pool. Green plants grew in abundance. Three ceiling fans moved lazily overhead.

"I assume you brought a résumé?" the butler inquired.

"Well, kind of." Summer handed her envelope to him. "It's pretty dorky. I mean, I don't exactly have a lot of companion experience, unless you count, you know, just hanging out with people."

He smiled. "Hanging out," he repeated, as if he'd never actually tried the phrase. "I shall pass this along." Chuckling under his breath, he left her alone.

"Excellent interview technique, Summer," she muttered. "Impress them with your total dweebness right up front."

She gazed around the room, then peeked into the adjacent living room. There was something sterile about the house. It didn't have the debris of daily life about it—magazines, letters, photos of family members, dust, confusion, and clutter. Or maybe really rich people didn't make messes. Maybe they just had them removed by specially trained anticlutter SWAT teams.

"Ms. Smith?"

Summer spun around. A young woman, maybe just a few years older than Summer, stood in the doorway. She had short curly hair and thickly lashed eyes. She was wearing a crisp white uniform. "Oh, hi. I wasn't snooping. Just . . . you know. Okay, I was snooping."

"I'm Juanita Rodriguez. We spoke on the phone."

Summer shook her hand. "Somehow I

thought you'd be older. I mean, you're a nurse, right?"

"LPN. Licensed Peon and Nobody. Have a seat."

"Thanks."

"I looked over your résumé," Juanita said, settling into a rocker next to Summer.

"Pretty pathetic, huh?"

"Not entirely. Me, I can't imagine tackling triplets." She smiled coolly, eyeing Summer up and down with obvious curiosity. "Actually, Jared—he's my patient—seemed quite impressed when I showed it to him. He asked to interview you himself."

"Impressed?" Summer laughed.

"Go figure." Juanita leaned forward, lowering her voice. "I just wanted to prepare you. Jared's been going through a tough time from a rehab point of view. He's paralyzed from the waist down, and he suffered severe lacerations to his head, neck, and right hand. He's just now regaining the use of his vocal cords. He has to speak quietly, and you have to work to listen. It's like talking to someone with a very hoarse voice."

Summer nodded. "Is he still . . . you know . . . bandaged and stuff?"

"Most of his face is," Juanita said as she counted off the details on her fingers, "plus his right hand and his neck. And his right leg's in a cast. They need to put a new pin in his ankle soon."

Summer winced. "He must be in a lot of pain."

"As much emotional as physical. He's pretty much alone here. His family pays the bills, but that's all they do. It's a real shame." She blinked back tears. "The staff tries to be there for him, but I suggested a companion might be a good idea. Jared's been reluctant to go ahead, but I finally placed the ad anyway."

She stood, cocking her head at Summer, still sizing her up. "So. I just wanted you to know what you may be getting yourself into. By the way, it's live-in if you want it. There's a whole wing for the staff."

"I have an apartment," Summer said. "I just want a normal nine-to-five kind of job."

Juanita shook her head. "Let me tell you something, Summer. There is nothing at all normal about this job."

Summer watched her leave. She moved purposefully, like someone on a tight deadline. Summer had the feeling Juanita didn't think she was up to the job.

A few moments later, as a big wheelchair slowly rolled into view, Summer wondered if maybe Juanita was right.

18

The Invisible Man

Sitting in the chair, erect, almost stiff, was a slender figure in a denim shirt. A white blanket was draped over his legs, one of which was in a cast. His right hand was wrapped in bandages nearly as thick as a boxing glove.

But it was his face—or what she could see of it—that made Summer's stomach lurch. It was swathed in so much white gauze that only his eyes, his ears, and part of the back of his head were visible.

Like a mummy, she thought. Trapped.

Summer tried not to react. She looked him directly in the eye, went over, and took his left hand.

"It's nice to meet you, Jared," she said. "I'm Summer Smith."

His tight grip surprised her because he appeared so frail. He looked up at her. Staring out from the white bandages, his dark eyes were startling, like a snowman's coal eyes.

"Summer. What a wonderful name." His voice was like a whispering stream over gravel. He studied her hand and made a noise that might have been a laugh but sounded more like a cough. "Good upper arm strength," he quoted from her résumé. "I like that."

Summer smiled. "I lifted a lot of trays."

A pause followed. He stared at her blatantly. From anyone else it would have been rude, but Summer didn't mind—maybe because she was staring too.

"Well, I'll leave you two," the nurse said. "Buzz me if you need anything, Jared."

"Thanks, Juanita."

Juanita gave a nod to Summer. "It was nice meeting you, Summer."

"You too."

Jared waited until Juanita had closed the door behind her. "Juanita's great. But very protective," he said. "So. You live here on the key?" His voice came slow and hushed, like air hissing from a tire.

Summer nodded. "Right in Old Town. An apartment in a Victorian house."

"Roommates?"

"My friend Marquez and my cousin Diana."

He paused, nodding, as if this information required some time to digest.

"Family?"

She noticed he spoke briefly, as if long sentences tired him. Maybe they did. With all those tight bandages, his lips could probably barely move.

"In Minnesota. That's where I'm from. Bloomington. The Mall of America's there." She rolled her eyes. She was babbling again. She always babbled when she was uncomfortable.

Jared appeared to smile, though it was hard to tell. It seemed to be less a full-fledged smile than a slight shift of the bandages surrounding his mouth.

"Boyfriend?"

Summer hesitated. "Um, yes."

"I'm not surprised."

She stared at her hands.

"Sorry. None of my business."

"No, that's okay. I'm engaged," Summer said. "His name is Seth. I had a ring, but it's temporarily vanished. At least I hope it's temporary."

Jared moved a little in his chair, wincing with the effort. He took such a long time to speak that Summer found herself trying to guess his next words.

"He's very lucky," he said finally.

"Well, that's debatable," she said with a shrug, "but thanks."

"So. Juanita told you the duties?"

"A little bit. Running errands, reading, that sort of thing."

"Chess?"

"Um, I don't play, I'm afraid. But I'd love to learn. And I'm great at poker."

"Movies?"

"I love movies. TV too."

He was staring again. She felt a little like a painting that had just been unveiled.

"Questions?"

"Well, hours, pay, all that."

"What hours do you want?"

"I guess like any regular job. Nine to five. Although," she added with a smile, "if you could make it ten to six, that'd be cool. I have this tendency to oversleep."

"Make your own hours."

"Really? Wow. Well, okay, but I'm flexible. Like if you wanted to go down to the beach and watch the sunrise or something, I could set my alarm." She flushed. Maybe he couldn't leave the house. "Is that something you could do? Go outside?"

He moved his head—a nod, she thought. "We have a specially equipped van."

"I was thinking we could just, you know, go out in the garden or maybe walk down the street. I could push your wheelchair—"

"It's electric."

"Oh. Well, then, maybe I could ride with you." She laughed, then wondered again if she'd put her foot in her mouth. "I'm sorry. I guess I'm not sure what to say."

"You're doing fine," he said. "How's twenty an hour to start?"

"Twenty dollars? An *hour*?"

"Okay, twenty-five."

"That's like . . . wow. That's more than minimum wage by a long shot."

"It's not an easy job." For the first time Jared looked away, past Summer to the blue-green waves. "Does this . . . disgust . . . ?"

Summer hesitated. At first she thought he'd said "discuss." Then she realized with a start what he meant: Did this job disgust her? Did *he* disgust her?

"Oh, no," she exclaimed. "Why would you even think that? You were hurt in an accident.

Why would I feel anything but . . ." She clutched at the air, searching for the right word. Not *pity*, that wasn't right. "Why would I feel anything but compassion? It could just as easily be me in that wheelchair as you."

"I don't think so," he said in a barely audible voice. He looked at her. His eyes seemed even darker. She wondered if they had tears in them. "Are you sure?"

"Wait a minute. Are you offering me the job?"

"I'd be grateful if you'd take it."

Summer grinned. "So when do I start?"

"Soon. Please."

She went to him and shook his hand, and then she saw for certain that he was crying.

19

Truth or Dare

Diver opened the door even before Caroline could knock. She was wearing a pink dress, something frilly that Marquez would never have been caught dead in. When she sashayed past him into Austin's living room, she left a flowery scent in her wake.

"You might want to close the door," she advised, settling on the couch, feet demurely crossed at the ankles. "I assume we're alone?"

"Austin's at work."

"Sit, sit. We have so much to discuss, Paul."

Diver leaned back against the door, arms crossed over his bare chest. "Just say it, Caroline."

"Jeez, you've turned into such a sourpuss.

155

Course, you always were a little . . . odd." She batted her eyelids. "Still, who knew you'd fill out so nicely? I might have paid more attention to you if I'd known."

"What do you want from me?"

Caroline tapped her finger on her chin. "Not a man to mince words, are you? Like my daddy. He's a lawyer, did you know that? I had one of the clerks at his office do a little fishin' for me—bein' the boss's baby girl does have its advantages—and I came up with the juiciest little tidbits about you, Paul."

"Such as?"

Caroline pulled several pages of faxes from her purse. "Well, for starters, there's an outstanding warrant for your arrest, but then you knew that." She glanced up at him. "Arson, murder, you name it. And here I always thought of you as an underachiever."

"I didn't do it, Caroline." His voice sounded distant and hollow, as if someone else were saying the words in a far-off room.

"Hmm. That's going to take a little convincing, isn't it, Paul? What with the flammable liquid all over the place—"

"What liquid?" Diver demanded.

"The police found traces of a solvent that could have been used to start the fire." She consulted her papers, biting her lower lip in concentration. "Nothing conclusive, apparently, but still . . ." She shook her head, smiling sympathetically. "It doesn't look good."

"He was refinishing some furniture on the porch," Diver murmured. "Maybe that was it."

"Could be. But then there's the other matter of your history."

"What history?"

"You know. All those pesky domestic calls to the house." Caroline put her hand to her chest. "I can still remember police cars showin' up at all hours. My mama would look out the window and say, 'Paul's daddy's havin' a bad day again.'" She lowered her voice. "And that time your mama went with the police, her eye as black as night—I tell you, I will never forget it till the day I die. We were just little kids then. Maybe you don't even remember."

Diver clenched his hands. He remembered, all right.

"But then, even after she died, the way your daddy would take his hand to you! My Lord, he had a temper." She set the papers aside. "It's only natural he would come to a sorry end. Frankly, I don't blame you one bit."

"I didn't kill him," Diver said, but even as he said it he had a flash of the fire behind him, receding from view as he ran like he'd never run before, his feet bare on the dewy lawn, his head bleeding. Running away. His father's screams had been drowned out by the sounds of the fire devouring everything in its path.

What he should have said was, "I don't remember killing him."

"Paul? You look a little pale."

Diver went to the kitchen and splashed water on his face. He wondered if he was going to be sick.

As he dried his face with a paper towel, Austin's phone rang. "I'll get it," Caroline volunteered sweetly.

"Don't!" Diver cried, lunging for the receiver. But it was too late.

"Hello?" Caroline said. She looked over at Diver. "Yes, he's here. Just a moment."

Diver grabbed the phone away.

"Diver? It's Summer."

"This isn't a good time, Summer."

"Who was that? The accent sounded familiar. Is that Caroline?"

"Yeah. She was just leaving."

Summer paused. "Look, I need to talk to you about Marquez. She says she's not going to counseling tomorrow. I thought if we got together—"

"Maybe later."

"Diver," Summer said sternly, "I know you aren't thrilled about having me in your life. I'm not thrilled about it either. But you're the one who said we had to work together to keep an eye on Marquez."

"I know." Diver glanced at Caroline. "Why don't you come over in half an hour?"

"I can't. I might run into Austin."

"Fine. I'll meet you at Surfin' Sam's, that little restaurant on the water. Half an hour."

"Good. Hey, you okay?"

"Yeah. Never better."

He hung up the phone. "Your sister?" Caroline inquired. "I've been meaning to get together with her. I'm sure she'd love to hear me reminisce about you as a kid. All the time she missed . . . it's a real tragedy, your being kidnapped and all. What a life you've had."

"How do you know about that?"

"Blythe told me. She heard it from someone at work who knows Marquez and Summer. It fit together nicely, once I had all the pieces." Caroline clucked her tongue. "Very movie-of-the-week, really. At least you had the good sense to be kidnapped by someone with big bucks."

"What are you talking about? They didn't have any money."

"Oh, but that's where you're wrong, Paul." Caroline waved her faxes in the air. "Mind if I get a drink? The heat here is just wilting me."

She poured herself a glass of water and drank it slowly, letting him wait. "See, it turns out your mean ol' daddy had a big stash of money. Guess there was a lot of insurance on your mama—what did she die of, anyway?"

"Cancer."

"Well, he made a killing, pardon the pun, and you, Paul—Diver, I mean—are the only heir." She shook her head. "Darn the luck, though. You go to claim the money, and sure as night follows day, they'll arrest your pretty little butt for murder. Isn't life funny sometimes?"

Diver sat down. He no longer trusted his legs. He felt he should say something, but there was nothing left to say. He'd been running from the truth for years. The truth always had a way of catching up with you, though.

"So what's your point, Caroline?" he asked wearily.

"Well, you can see how awkward my position is. I mean, I *have* to turn you in, Paul. It's my duty as a citizen." She tapped her finger on her chin. "Of course, if we went in together and I told them a nice little story about how I woke up that night and looked out my bedroom window, how I saw you try to save your daddy by runnin' bravely back into the flames . . . well, you get the idea. I could turn you into a hero, Paul. They'd drop the charges, probably give you the key to the city."

"And your motivation for this would be . . . ?"

"Eighty percent of the insurance money." Her voice had lost its southern sweetness. "I was going to take it all, but I'm a good Christian. And I believe in giving even the worst sinner a second chance."

"This is blackmail."

"Go ahead and complain to the police. I dare you."

"They'll ask you why you didn't tell them all this earlier," Diver pointed out.

She shrugged. "Post-traumatic stress, isn't that what you call it? I'll tell them I blotted the whole awful episode right out of my mind."

She sat back against the couch and checked her watch. "So, what'll it be? The gas chamber or a ticker-tape parade? Seems like a pretty easy choice to me."

Diver closed his eyes. Sometimes, when he

concentrated hard enough, he could still feel the heat of the fire sweeping toward him, enraged, like a living thing.

He opened his eyes. "You're right, Caroline," he said. "It's a pretty easy choice, all right."

20

True Confessions at Surfin' Sam's

"Have a burger. It's on me," Summer said to Diver as he slipped into the chair across from her. "I'm officially employed. Not only that, I'm overpaid."

Diver said something, but she couldn't hear him. Surfin' Sam's, a beachfront burger joint that was little more than a large shack, was filled to the brim with tourists and locals. Most were in bathing suits, half were toting surfboards, and all were rowdy.

"What did you say?" Summer asked loudly.

"Congratulations."

"Thanks." She took a sip of her Coke. "Diver, what's wrong? You look sick."

"Flu, I think. I'm okay."

163

Summer reached across the table and felt his head. "You sure?"

"Positive, Mom."

"Fry?"

"I'm not hungry."

"This is totally none of my business," Summer said, "so you can tell me to back off, but what was Caroline doing at your place?"

Diver tapped his fingers on the table, glaring at her. "Back off."

"Oh, come on, Diver. You know darn well Marquez will tell me anyway."

"It's really not that interesting."

"Humor me."

Diver sighed. "Caroline was right, it turns out. We *were* neighbors way back when. Only it was when we were really little, and she had the place wrong. It was in North Carolina. My folks—my other folks—lived there for a while. So did her family."

"So who's Paul?"

"She got the name wrong too. Between you and me, Caroline's not all that tightly wrapped." He shrugged. "Paul was this guy who lived down the block from us. A real bully. Used to terrorize us both." He gave a lame laugh. "She stopped by, we reminisced. I think . . . you know, maybe she was coming on to me."

164

"Wouldn't surprise me. Every girl at Bloomington High wanted to be my friend while you were going to school there. You made me very popular. Temporarily." She pushed her plate aside. "You want my advice?"

He smiled grimly. "No."

"Whatever you do, don't tell Marquez about Caroline. The last thing she needs to worry about right now is the possibility of losing you."

"Why would she lose me?" Diver asked sharply.

"To another girl," Summer said. "There are lots of Carolines out there, lying in wait to prey on naive, unsuspecting guys like you. Why else?"

The waitress buzzed past and handed Diver a menu. "Thanks, he said, "but I'm just passing through."

"Too bad for me," she replied with a wink.

Summer rolled her eyes. "I rest my case."

"Look," Diver said, leaning close, "I need you to make Marquez understand that she has to take better care of herself. It's her responsibility."

"I've tried," Summer said. "I was hoping you could get through to her."

Diver combed his fingers through his hair. "I'm not the best one to give lectures on responsibility. I have a tendency to walk out when things get tough."

"At least you leave polite notes behind," Summer said. "Allow me to quote in full: 'I'm sorry.' No greeting, no signature. Succinct, to the point, no unnecessary emotion."

She saw the pain in his eyes and almost regretted her sarcastic tone. They were there to talk about Marquez, not to reopen old wounds.

"I need you to promise me something, Summer," Diver said. "No matter how you feel about me, you'll always be there for Marquez, right?"

"Of course I will. She's my best friend."

He leaned back, studying her. "It's easy for you," he said.

"What?"

"Sticking around for people. Loyalty."

Summer gave a rueful laugh. "Not always. Ask Seth."

"Still, when you say you'll stick by Marquez and get her through this, I know you mean it. If I said it, it would be just . . . words."

Summer gazed at her brother. Diver was talking in riddles. He was good at that. Of course, he was also good at talking to pelicans. He was like an onion: peel away one layer of mystery and there was always another one waiting.

"Diver," she said softly, "are you sure you're okay?"

"I'm always okay. You know that."

Against her better judgment, she reached across the table and squeezed his hand.

"Have you forgotten you hate me?"

"I don't hate you, Diver. You just . . . disappointed me, is all."

"It's a habit of mine."

"That's water under the bridge. The real problem is Marquez. I'll talk to her, make her see how worried you are. Maybe I can get through to her with a guilt trip—I'll say you're a wreck and that she owes you."

"She doesn't owe me. I owe her. She's the first person I've ever really let myself love since . . . you know. Since I was little."

"Since Mom and Dad," Summer said softly, waiting for the inevitable clarification, the "Jack and Kim."

But Diver simply nodded. "And since you."

The moment hung suspended in time, floating between them like a fragile soap bubble. Neither moved or spoke for fear it would burst.

At last Diver pushed back his chair. "Well, I need to go."

"I know you're worried about Marquez," Summer said. "But she'll be fine. You love her, and I love her. And she can count on us, right?"

"Right," Diver whispered, speaking not to her, it seemed, but to some secret part of himself.

21

It's Always So Nice to Get Mail

When Summer got back to the apartment, it was empty. There was a note from Seth on the counter:

Hi, Summer—
Marquez is at work, Diana's at her volunteer thing, I'm out ring shopping. Back from Woolworth soon. I love you.

Summer smiled. She went to her room and changed into a pair of cutoffs and a T-shirt. The room was a mess. Apparently Diana had been on another reorganizing frenzy. There were boxes everywhere, papers on the floor, clothes on her bed and on Summer's.

Summer sighed. Maybe the problem was that Diana had grown up with a maid to clean up after her. Summer had to clear off a place on her bed just to sit down.

She felt like napping. She wasn't tired, really, but she wanted to sleep away the images that kept coming back to her, haunting her mind: Austin the night before, drunk, depressed, in pain because of her. Jared that day, trapped in a mangled body, willing to pay a stranger to be his friend. And Diver just now, unreachable as always, trying nonetheless to say he loved her.

At least that was what she thought he'd been trying to say. With Diver, it was difficult to ever really know.

She thought of Seth, out buying a ring at Woolworth, and smiled. Sweet, reliable, solid Seth. Sometimes she didn't realize how lucky she was. At least with Seth she always knew where she stood.

She pushed back her sheets, tossing aside more of Diana's stuff. She should have known better than to share a room with her cousin. This bedroom was the size of Diana's old closet in her former house. *One* of her closets.

Summer grabbed a box of postcards and odds

and ends off her pillow. Underneath it was a letter. She tossed it in the box and shoved the box onto Diana's side of the room.

With a sigh, she crawled under her sheets and closed her eyes.

Her eyes flew open.

Seth, the letter had said. The name had been written in Diana's careful, perfect handwriting.

Why would Diana have been writing Seth?

Summer climbed out of bed and went over to the box. She fished out the note and began to read.

1/14

Seth:

This is my fifth letter to you. You haven't received any of them because I haven't sent any of them, and I probably won't send this one either. I'm not used to embarrassing myself, and I'm not used to being the one doing the chasing. Face it, I'm used to guys coming after me. This is a new experience. I'm sure you're smiling to yourself in that smug way you sometimes have.

But anyway, here goes. I know you

think what happened between us New Year's Eve was a terrible mistake.

Summer paused. She went over to her bed and sat down on the edge, clutching the letter to her chest. New Year's Eve.

What happened between us New Year's Eve.

She plunged to the letter's finish, like a reader who just had to know how the story ended.

The point is, I've always been in love with you, Seth, and I just never had the nerve

That was it. No signature, no finish.

Summer read the letter again, this time taking in each word. When she was done, she did not cry or tear up the letter or crumple it. She put it back in the box.

She went to the closet and pulled out her battered old suitcase. Carefully she packed: tops, jeans, shorts, a couple of skirts, underwear.

She went to the bathroom and got her brush, hair dryer, shampoo, and conditioner. Toothbrush, floss, Tampax.

She zipped up the suitcase. Her hands were not trembling. Her lip was not quivering. She felt strangely, eerily calm, the unnatural quiet in the eye of a hurricane.

She got a phone number from her purse, then found Diana's cell phone and dialed.

"Juanita?" she said calmly. "It's Summer Smith. I've changed my mind about the live-in position."

When she hung up, she found a pen and a notepad. The first note was to Marquez.

Marquez—
I am at 1304 Naples Avenue in Eden Shores.
Please come see me. Promise you'll go to counseling tomorrow. Diver is really worried.
Don't worry about me. I'm fine.

She got a fresh piece of paper. She thought for a while. At last she wrote:

Seth and Diana—
I know everything. Do not try to get in touch with me.

Succinct, to the point, no unnecessary emotion. It was a note to make Diver proud.

22

Summer Returns

When the doorbell rang, he was already waiting, his left hand tightly clutching the arm of his wheelchair.

"Shall I, sir?" Stan, the butler, asked.

"Please."

The door swung wide, and there she was: the long tanned legs, the hair like yellow silk.

"Summer," he said.

Her face was drawn, pale. "Thank you for letting me come, Jared."

She stepped inside. Stan took her bag.

"The west wing, sir?"

"What color do you like?" he asked Summer. "Blue, yellow, cream? Your pick."

"I don't care," she said softly.

"Blue, then," he said, and Stan headed upstairs.

He held out his good hand. "I'm glad you'll be staying here with us," he said. "It'll be good to have you."

She took his hand and nodded. Her eyes were glassy. She looked as though she weren't quite sure where she was.

"I had a change of plans," she said.

"I understand."

Juanita came down the stairs. She glanced at Summer's hand in his disapprovingly, but he held on a little longer.

"Well, this certainly is a surprise," Juanita said. "But of course we're pleased to have you join the staff. Will you be having dinner with us this evening?"

"I . . . no. I'm not hungry, thank you."

"I wish you would," he said.

Summer looked at him. "We'll see," she said.

"You're all right?" Juanita asked. "You look a bit under the weather."

"I had a, um, a situation I had to deal with." Summer twisted the Kleenex she was carrying. "I'm okay, though."

"Perhaps after you're settled we can meet to discuss your duties," Juanita suggested. "I thought a regular schedule might be easier for Jared—reading in the morning, time in the garden in the afternoon, things like that. Perhaps we can put together an activities list."

"That would be fine."

"Juanita," he said, "let her rest. She just got here, and she's obviously had a hard day."

Juanita shrugged. "Fine. We'll meet in the morning, then. Nine sharp?"

"Nine," Summer said flatly.

"I'll be in the kitchen, Jared, if you need me."

"I'll be fine," he said. "Summer and I will be fine."

"All right, then. If you're sure." Juanita marched off.

Summer stood quietly in the foyer next to his chair. A shaft of light through the window made her seem to glow. Or maybe it was just his imagination seeing something that wasn't really there.

"Why don't we go out to the porch?" he suggested.

Summer blinked, momentarily confused, a stranger in a foreign land. "Oh," she said, "all right." She gestured toward the door. "After you."

He guided his chair to the porch. She followed behind him.

When they got there, she went to the

screened window and stared out at the ocean.

"So something happened," he said, hoping he sounded gentle, not too prying.

She nodded.

"I'm sorry."

She turned. "Don't be. What happened . . . it's nothing like what happened to you. A small thing, really."

"Matters of the heart are never small."

He said it in that flat, asthmatic way he could not avoid. The way an old man would talk, waging a battle in his throat to form each word. Talking made him terribly tired, but he so wanted to talk to her.

She sat beside him. He could smell her, an alive, sweet scent that made him ache for all he had lost.

"How did you know it was a matter of the heart?" she asked. She smiled a little when she said the word *heart*.

"I had a few . . . matters of my own, before." Instantly he wished he hadn't made reference to the time before. It sounded self-pitying. The last thing he wanted was Summer's pity. "And I could tell. Your eyes look so sad."

She glanced down as if she was embarrassed. "My boyfriend and my cousin. I found out they had a . . . relationship I didn't know about."

He looked away, too, letting it all sink in, word by word. The quiet seemed unbearable. He knew he should say something, anything.

"You must feel very betrayed."

"I trusted them. I thought I was the one making all the mistakes, and then it turned out—" A catch in her voice made her stop—a sob, but not quite. "I'm sorry. To sit here, feeling sorry for myself, when you've gone through so much more . . . what a jerk I am."

He tried to shrug, which was hard, and wished again for the simple ways people communicated—a wave of the hand, a wink, a nudge. All lost to him, at least for the time being.

"Physical pain is different. You can fight it more easily because it's . . ." He didn't know where to go. He hadn't tried to talk about it before.

"I think I know what you mean," Summer said. "Because it's a thing outside yourself, in a way. Emotional pain is inside you. Is that it?"

He nodded. It was so good to talk to her. It was as though the electricity had gone off in a violent storm and now, in the space of a moment, the power was on again, the lights worked, the phone was connected. He was part of the world once more.

She was there in his house. There, after so long. After so much silence.

"For him to hurt you like this, he must have truly lost his way," he said. "He must have forgotten what matters. It can happen. Even when you don't mean to, it's easy to lose track of what's most important. . . ."

He could see the look of confusion in her eyes. He was saying too much too fast. He was scaring her—with his words, but no doubt with his physical self as well. He sometimes forgot how frightening he was. He'd had all the mirrors removed long ago.

"I think maybe I need to lie down," Summer said. "Would that be okay?"

"Of course. Your room is up the stairs, the first one on the right. If you need anything, ask one of the staff."

"Maybe later I could read something to you," Summer said shyly. "If you'd like."

"You rest tonight. There's plenty of time for that."

"It might be good. It might take my mind off everything." She stood. "No romances, though."

He laughed, or at least tried to. It had been so long, his face didn't remember how to laugh anymore.

180

"Well . . . I'll go unpack."

She paused at the door. She was looking at him with pity, he knew that, and yet it pleased him just to have such a beautiful woman looking at him at all.

"Have you read *Huckleberry Finn?*"

"Not in a long time."

"Maybe we'll start with that, Jared."

He watched her slowly climb the stairs. For a moment he thought he could hear her voice lingering in the air, saying the other name, saying "Adam."

It had been so long since he'd heard her say it.

Maybe someday, when he had the courage, he would ask her to say it again.

23

Diver Says Good-bye

Austin crossed the lawn wearily. His brain throbbed indignantly. After the abuse he'd heaped on it the night before, he couldn't really blame it.

He was almost to the porch when Diver emerged from the apartment. His sleeping bag and backpack were slung over his shoulder.

"Hey, where are you off to?" Austin asked.

Diver looked uncomfortable. "Thought maybe I'd do a little camping for a couple of days," he said. "You know, adjust my *wa* and all that."

"Does your *wa* realize you just started a new job?"

"Yeah, well . . . the people at work, they're cool with it."

"You're not moving out because I made a drunken ass of myself in front of your sister last night, are you?"

Diver smiled. "No. I didn't even know you'd made a drunken ass of yourself."

"I have no idea what happened. I mean, I'm a rational guy. I'm not some slobbering, incoherent fool who'd crash a party and completely humiliate himself. Or so I thought."

"I saw Summer a while ago. She didn't even mention it, Austin."

Austin couldn't help feeling a little disappointed. "Nothing?"

"Nothing. Hey, I gotta get going."

"Far be it from me to interfere, but you're okay, right, man?"

"Yeah. I just feel like taking a little break from the real world." Diver strode away. At the curb he stopped. "If you see Summer—"

"That's not too likely, I'm afraid."

"Well, if you do, tell her something for me, okay?"

"Sure. You name it."

"Tell her she was right about me all along."

He was lucky. There was a Greyhound leaving at seven for Miami.

He took a seat near the back. The bus was almost empty: a couple of kids, a guy with tattoos weaving up his forearms, a grandmother type. The bus smelled of diesel fumes. The seat was sticky.

Diver felt right at home.

He'd done the dog a lot the last few years. Mostly he'd hitched, but every now and then he'd come into some cash and taken the high road. He liked the anonymous feel of the bus. People left you alone. They all had their problems—tearful departures, uncertain destinations, missed connections.

The bus growled to life, and the door squealed shut. They backed out onto the tiny main street that bisected Old Town. It was packed with tourists: families on rented bicycles, in-line skaters, couples strolling hand in hand and eating ice cream while they window-shopped.

It took Diver a minute to realize they were going to pass right by Marquez's apartment. As it came into view he considered ducking. But the windows were tinted, and no one would expect to see him there.

Then he saw her.

She was standing in front of Jitters, her waitress apron over her shoulder, a cup of coffee in her hand. She was watching the crowds pass by.

For a moment she looked at the bus, taking it in without knowing. The breeze moved her hair. She pushed it back with a gesture both impatient and graceful.

Diver reached into his backpack. He found the note he'd written. It was long by his standards, even rambling. And it was full of passion, full of pleas for forgiveness.

As if he deserved any.

He crumpled it up. He was glad he hadn't left it for her, and now he knew he wouldn't ever send it.

This time he understood that no note could ever undo the pain he was causing.

This time he knew he could not be forgiven.

You didn't walk out on the people you loved. You didn't run when things got complicated.

Summer didn't.

He did.

The bus turned, and he looked back one last time. The street was bathed in the orange light of sunset, erasing Marquez, blinding him.

The sky, he thought, looked as if it were on fire.

About the Author

After Katherine Applegate graduated from college, she spent time waiting tables, typing (badly), watering plants, wandering randomly from one place to the next with her boyfriend, and just generally wasting her time. When she grew sufficiently tired of performing brain-dead minimum-wage work, she decided it was time to become a famous writer. Anyway, a writer. Writing proved to be an ideal career choice, as it involved neither physical exertion nor uncomfortable clothing, and required no social skills.

Ms. Applegate has written over sixty books under her own name and a variety of pseudonyms. She has no children, is active in no organizations, and has never been invited to address a joint session of Congress. She does, however, have an evil, foot-biting cat named Dick, and she still enjoys wandering randomly from one place to the next with her boyfriend.